Discard

Notr   ool

the sweetheart of prosper county

the sweetheart of prosper county

by jill s. alexander

SQUARE
FISH

Feiwel and Friends
New York, NY

SQUARE
FISH

An Imprint of Macmillan

THE SWEETHEART OF PROSPER COUNTY.
Copyright © 2009 by Jill S. Alexander.
All rights reserved. Distributed in Canada by
H.B. Fenn and Company Ltd. Printed in July 2010 in the
United States of America by R. R. Donnelley & Sons Company,
Harrisonburg, Virginia. For information, address Square Fish,
175 Fifth Avenue, New York, NY 10010.

Square Fish and the Square Fish logo are trademarks of Macmillan and
are used by Feiwel and Friends under license from Macmillan.

Library of Congress Cataloging-in-Publication Data

Alexander, Jill S.
The Sweetheart of Prosper County / Jill S. Alexander. p. cm.
Summary: In a small East Texas town, fourteen-year-old Austin sets
out to win a ride in the next parade and, in the process, grows in her
understanding of friendship, faces down bullies and prejudices,
and helps her widowed mother through her mourning.
ISBN: 978-0-312-54857-5
[1. Self-confidence—Fiction.   2. Bullies—Fiction.   3. Grief—Fiction.
4. Mothers and daughters—Fiction.   5. Friendship—Fiction.
6. Prejudices—Fiction.   7. Future Farmers of America—Fiction.
8. Texas—Fiction.]   I. Title. PZ7.M478414337Hoo 2009
[Fic]—dc22   2008034757

Originally published in the United States by Feiwel and Friends
Square Fish logo designed by Filomena Tuosto
First Square Fish Edition: 2010
Design by Barbara Grzeslo
www.squarefishbooks.com
10 9 8 7 6 5 4 3 2 1

LEXILE 710L

For my husband, Jon, who never gave up
on the girl from Winfield, Texas.

the sweethe♥rt of prosper county

1
a hood ornament
in the
no-jesus christmas parade

Sundi Knutt had a blue-ribbon-winning sow, a deer hunting license, and a mound of cleavage. She rode on the hood of Josh Whatley's daddy's four-wheel drive Super-Cab Ford. The Future Farmers of America chapter hung posters on each side door glitter-glued with FFA SWEET-HEART in all caps. The truck was mirror white, and Sundi, stuffed in a strapless red velvet dress trimmed with real, white rabbit fur, waved to each side of the crowd as the truck poked around the downtown square.

"Hey!" A voice hollered toward Sundi. It was Dean Ottmer, standing in the middle of his spit-and-scratch so-called friends with his baseball cap on backwards. The cap pushed his straw hair down into his eyes, making him look like a short sheepdog. "Mrs. Claus called and she wants her outfit back!" His gang laughed and high-fived each other. Sundi just rode on, smiling and waving. Being a sweetheart must give a girl that kind of confidence.

"She looks like a cherry plopped on top of a DQ soft-serve sundae." Maribel sucked on a candy cane, watching Sundi roll by.

Maribel and I weren't parade royalty. We were just taking up space on the curb, waving back at the sweethearts, hoping to stay off Dean Ottmer's radar.

"She looks more like an ornament to me," I said. "Just hook a paper clip on her head and hang her from a Christmas tree."

The truck inched along and so did Sundi's dress. She stopped waving long enough to hook her thumbs under the fur and tug and pull the top up, but it looked about as pointless as trying to carry a couple of big water balloons in a handkerchief.

The Big Wells High School cheerleading squad came flipping behind the FFA Sweetheart. The Roughnecks' mascot, a girl hidden under an oversized man head with a permanent scowl, threw handfuls of plastic-wrapped candy canes into the crowd. Folks were scrambling around trying to catch them and scooping them off the ground.

Maribel stepped off the curb, picked up a fistful, and shoved them into her purse—a yellow mesh shoulder bag bearing the unibrowed likeness of Frida Kahlo and the declaration *I Paint My Own Reality* on the side.

"You'd think they were throwing money," I said.

She tucked her black hair behind her ear. "Can't hear you!"

The school band was going by, tooting and banging out

"Jingle Bells." I felt bad for Lewis Fortenberry. He marched in the back row with his tuba. Lewis was knock-kneed, and his blue uniform pants were too small and too snug around his big, flat butt. He looked like somebody squeezed his legs together and the fat parts just spread out over the top of his belt.

"Austin, he's got bad muffin top," Maribel whispered.

Dean Ottmer stepped off the curb and got behind the band. He had his T-shirt tucked into his jeans, and his jeans pulled down below his crack. He pinched his butt cheeks together and pretend-marched a few feet behind Lewis. Dean's buddies clapped and yelled, "DEAN-O, DEAN-O, DEAN-O, DEAN-O."

Lord, Jesus! I threw my head back, looking for some help from above. *Dean Ottmer is present.* Momma said to pray the problem, not the outcome. She said that in the Bible, Mary doesn't pray for Jesus to bring wine; she just told him they were out, then he gave them a flowing river of wine. Momma said to tell Jesus the problem and let Him solve it in His way in His time. But I added anyway, *Ninth grade has been rough, and I've got three and a half years of high school left.* And one more time in case He missed it, *Dean Ottmer is present.*

I opened my eyes. Dean was still there—the biggest mouth in the crowd lining Main Street. The whole town and half of Prosper County had turned out for the annual Big Wells Christmas parade. A small-town social event. As big a draw as Friday night football and Sunday morning church.

Some burly man with a four-year-old on his shoulders decided he could get a better view if he stood in front of me, so Maribel and I had to move. Mayor Nesmith's float was coming by; we wanted to be in the front for that. He had been mayor of Big Wells for three years, and every year he had the best parade float, and handpicked kids off the curb and out of the crowd to ride on it. Maribel and I were hoping this year was our turn. Mayor Nesmith was up for re-election; I felt sure he'd load his float up with kids.

As Mayor Nesmith's float got closer, downtown Big Wells began to smell like a movie theater.

"Wow!" Maribel drew in a long sniff. "It's a popcorn buffet."

And it was. Mayor Nesmith's float was a spanking-new, red eighteen-wheeler with a flatbed, lowboy trailer. The trailer had two popcorn machines on each end, a Christmas tree with the White family dressed fancy and stringing popcorn garlands — Mrs. White had been Miss Texas and her perfect twins had her silky blond hair — and a few veterans dressed in their military uniforms walking along handing out bags of popcorn. "Run Run Rudolph" blasted from the float. Tiffany Smoot, the high school dance team captain, and Marvelle Jones, the first male, African-American cheerleader in Big Wells, performed a super-fast swing dance in the middle of the float. Two long banners hung from each side of the trailer: HAVE A HOT POPPIN' DOO-WOP CHRISTMAS.

Mayor Nesmith hopped out of the shiny red cab in a business suit, a red tie, and a Santa Claus hat. He gave

4

everyone a big, two-handed wave and walked toward Maribel and me, smiling directly at us.

"This is it, Maribel." I grabbed her arm. We stepped off the curb. "We're *finally* getting to ride in the Christmas parade."

Mayor Nesmith grabbed two bags of popcorn from one of the veterans and stiff-armed them at me and Maribel. We stopped in our tracks. He turned away from us and shook hands with the burly man. The little girl on the man's shoulders reached down toward the mayor. She had curly black hair and black patent-leather shoes and a shorty-short black satin dress with a white lace collar. She looked like a collectible doll sold in a box. A veteran wearing a starched white navy uniform put a stepladder by the truck's cab. Mayor Nesmith carried the little doll up the steps and posed her on the hood. She immediately began waving and smiling—side to side, side to side.

"A hood ornament!" I stepped back onto the curb and pulled a fistful of popcorn from the bag. "I haven't liked Nesmith since he took Jesus out of the parade."

In his first parade as mayor, Nesmith assembled a baby-Jesus-in-the-manger float. County folks loaned him a goat, two sheep, and a donkey. He borrowed a camel from the exotic animal farm by the interstate. The Methodists donated a young couple and their new baby. Mayor Nesmith rented a Roman soldier costume and stood in front of the manger scene waving. Less than a week later, the *Big Wells Tribune* ran an editorial on the separation of church and state, using the mayor and his float as the example. The paper quoted the mayor the next day as saying it was an honest mistake and that future Christmas parades would definitely not include Jesus.

"He gave Reese's out?" Maribel asked, hoping for some chocolate.

"No!" I yelled over "Rockin' Around the Christmas Tree." "I said 'JESUS OUT'!"

Nesmith's doo-wop vote float rolled slowly past, making sure everyone could read the huge sign stretched across the back of the trailer:

RE-ELECT
MAYOR VICTOR NESMITH

I heard a crowd of boys laughing and looked around. Dean Ottmer had a couple of his jerk friends locked elbow to elbow and standing off the curb—one brown-haired string bean stooge and one short dumpy guy with a candy cane in his mouth. Dean imitated Nesmith and strutted toward them—shoving each in the chest with half-empty popcorn bags. He shoved them again, then pointed and hee-hawed at me and Maribel. I pinched my lips together and made out like I didn't get that he was making fun of us, like I didn't even see him. But he was still there, still laughing, and still under my skin.

The United Hispanics of Texas cruised to a stop in front of us. The UHOT board members rode in an old Impala

6

convertible painted metallic brown with chrome rims and brown-trimmed, white leather seats. Daisy Flores, a senior and the UHOT *La Reina*, graced the hood.

"She is a daisy," I said. The sleeves of her yellow satin dress framed her brown face and eyes when she raised her arms to wave.

"Rrrrrrrrrrrrdddd!" Maribel hollered, trilling her *r*'s for everyone to hear.

She tried teaching me how to do that once, but I just spit a rain shower trying to say *arriba*. Everyone in the UHOT cruiser whistled back at Maribel, like they knew her personally, like she had some double life I knew nothing about.

Dean Ottmer and company belted out a Spanglish karaoke attempt at *"Feliz Navidad."* They made up Spanish-sounding words for the lyrics they didn't know.

"Good gravy!" Maribel rolled her eyes, blowing Dean off. "He just makes fun of everything."

Texanne Farhat, the Rodeo Club Sweetheart two years running, rode by on the hood of a 1970s Cadillac with real cow horns mounted on the car's grille.

"Those must've come off a big side of beef," Maribel said.

Texanne held the state record in barrel racing as a freshman and a sophomore. She wore a pink, wide-brimmed cowboy hat and huge grin. She had Bugs Bunny front teeth but didn't seem to care as she sat on that hood, waving and blowing kisses at the crowd.

"Hey!" Dean Ottmer was at it again. "I bet you could bite an apple through a picket fence!" Then he held two bent fingers in front of his top lip and waved real big with his other hand. Texanne covered her mouth with both hands, then blew double kisses, maybe even quadruple kisses, toward Dean. She took off her hat and drew big circles in the air with it, like a lasso. Then she yelled, "WHOOOOOP!" She had her very own cowgirl signature wave and holler, and Dean Ottmer meant nothing to her.

Maribel and I cracked up.

"What are you laughing at, *chestless*?" Dean flattened his palms and mashed them across the front of his shirt. "Austin, Texas"—Dean kept his palms flat against his chest—"the no-hill country."

Dang. It seemed like the whole crowded curb laughed—everyone except me and Maribel. I was nobody's sweetheart, and I didn't have a signature wave. And I had no car to ride off on when Dean Ottmer punched me with insults. I just stood on the curb with a greasy popcorn sack and a red face as the parade rolled by.

"Don't let him get to you, Austin." Maribel tried to make me feel better for the umpteenth time. "He's like E. coli—just contaminates everything he comes in contact with."

But this time Dean Ottmer had flipped my switch. No way could I spend the next three and a half years of high school being identified as "Austin Gray, you know, the girl who's the butt of Dean Ottmer's jokes." I had taken his smack since fourth grade and done nothing. Just like I

8

waited on the curb for someone to pull me into the parade instead of joining in on my own. I had to redefine myself in high school, become something other than Dean's punch line.

"That's it, Maribel," I said as Santa Claus rode by on the fire truck. "This is the last time I'm getting stuck on the curb with Dean-O the Jerk-O. No matter what I have to do, come next year, I'm going to be a hood ornament in the No-Jesus Christmas Parade."

a poultry plan

"Momma, I want a chicken for Christmas."

"Austin, you know we always have turkey, maybe some ham."

Gray's True Value Hardware store closed promptly every day at six, and Momma was counting the cash out of the register. She had a pencil stuck between the spikes of her short hair, and the sleeves on her black turtleneck pushed up to her elbows.

"Not to eat," I said. "I want one for competition. I'm going to join the Future Farmers of America next year. They teach agribusiness." Momma never argued against academics. "And they require that you have a project, to grow a crop or own livestock."

Momma's reading glasses hung on the end of her nose. She looked above the rectangles and blinked her eyes at Maribel. "I guess you'll need a goat?"

"Oh, no, ma'am," Maribel said. She was flipping through a *Quince Girl* magazine. "I'm signing up for culinary arts. The classroom has a full kitchen. We get to make cinnamon rolls out of canned biscuits. Besides, I don't care as much as Austin does about riding in the no-Jesus parade."

"Well, thanks, Miss Quinceañera, for clearing that up for us." Being Latina, Maribel had a cultural advantage to turning fifteen. "You know, not *everyone* gets their own official coming-out celebration when they have their next birthday." I straightened my denim miniskirt and hopped onto the counter.

Momma shoved stacks of bills into a bank bag and zipped it. "Austin, tell me you're not making important school choices based on a hood ride."

"I have to have an elective, and it may as well be one I can use," I said.

Momma and I kept no intentional secrets. She knew I was bent on getting in that Christmas parade. I hadn't told her why, probably because I didn't know how to word it. I was just tired of feeling less-than, tired of waving back and being passed by . . . and tired of being stuck on the curb with Dean Ottmer. I wanted to make a stand about who I am, not someone defined by Dean or anyone else.

"The fire chief comes in the store at least once a week." Momma grabbed a diet soda from the small refrigerator in her office, shutting the door with the toe of her boot. "I bet I could get him to let you and Maribel dress up like Nutcrackers or toys like Raggedy Ann dolls and walk with the fire truck in next year's parade."

"Raggedy Ann is NOT an icon of beauty and self-confidence, Momma," I pleaded. "She's an empty-headed rag doll, for crying out loud . . . and she has no ride! Besides," I added to clear up Momma's confusion, "the point is to be *me* in the parade—not me just dressed up as somebody else."

"We would get to pass out candy," Maribel added as she folded a corner of the magazine.

"Maribel, we are not going to be Raggedy Ann dolls. I want to wear a party dress, not a costume." I twisted my hair into a rope and held it on top of my head. "I want a prom queen updo from the hair salon in the mall, not braids. And I want a chance to ride high and show that I'm my own person, I'm somebody. Not some made-up character. AND I WANT A CHICKEN FOR CHRISTMAS!"

"Austin Gray." Momma flipped off the lights and set the store's alarm. "You *are* somebody, and even if you weren't, a champion yard bird wouldn't change your status."

"Look"—I felt the need to point out the facts to her— "Sundi Knutt entered that fat sow of hers in last year's county fair. It won first place and helped Sundi become the FFA Sweetheart. I checked the rules. The animal has to be in the contestant's care by April first in order to be judged at the county fair in June. There's a poultry division; I could easily take care of a chicken."

"Your chicken, your responsibility," Momma said as we stepped out of the store and into the night. "You'll have to pay some towards its food and shelter." She put one arm around me and the other around Maribel.

I looked down on the tips of Momma's spiky hair. She'd

always been petite, but somewhere between the eighth and ninth grades, I had shot past her.

"I need gift-wrapping help at the store every day next week since it's the week before Christmas. Minimum wage plus tips," she continued.

"I'm in," Maribel chimed. "I could use the money for my *quinceañera*. My sister will want to work, too. She'll be on break from nursing school."

Everyone in Maribel's family had jobs. Her father, Louis Sanchez, owned Sanchez Lawn Service. Her mother, Dolores, cleaned houses. Her older brother, Manuel, bused tables at The Hushpuppy, an all-you-can-eat catfish joint.

So Maribel, her sister Marilinda, and I began working the first Monday morning of our holiday break from school. Gray's True Value was the oldest store in the oldest building on the corner of the Big Wells town square. The plate-glass windows along the front rattled when the wind blew, the door slammed, or a car drove by too fast. The wood floor must have been at least a hundred years old; we knew the customers by the clopping of their work boots or the clicking of their heels. For four generations, my family had supplied Big Wells and the surrounding counties with all kinds of hardware: nails, horse tack, pocketknives, canning jars. When Supermart moved in, everyone said that Gray's True Value would be forced out of business. But they underestimated my momma. Before Supermart ever opened its doors, she split Gray's True Value down its wooden, center aisle — one half stayed hardware, the other half became housewares

13

and a bridal registry. Momma sold everything from cheese graters to crystal goblets. The Supermart didn't knock a dent in her business. Besides, they didn't even gift wrap.

"Austin." Momma stacked three crystal pitchers on the wrap table. "Wrap these separately for Mrs. Teaga den. She's waiting."

"You got it."

We had three choices of paper: plain brown, for those who liked the old-school hardware store look; green covered with tiny, gold pine trees; and a red-and-white candy cane stripe. Maribel, her sister Marilinda, and I each took a pitcher and a different wrap. We finished the gifts off with yarn bows and the Gray's True Value gold sticker.

"Thank you very much." I handed the wrapped packages to Mrs. Teagarden.

"Merry Christmas," she said. Then she handed me three five-dollar bills and patted my hand. Mrs. Teagarden, and every other blue-hair in town, pigeonholed me as Little Austin Gray. For them, I would always be eight years old — stuck being identified by the year my father died. "What are you asking St. Nick for this year?"

"A chicken." The line of customers in checkout chuckled. I didn't let that faze me. "I'm joining the FFA, and I plan on winning the Poultry Division at the fair."

"Well," Mrs. Teagarden said. "If you're anything like your poor momma, there's nothing you can't do if you set your mind on it."

Mrs. Teagarden just had to go there. She was probably

talking about my dead daddy. People always gave Momma backhanded compliments about being strong or hearty or hardworking, like it surprised them that she just didn't curl up in a ball of self-pity when he died.

In the six years since Daddy's death, I had learned to just let the comments go. Momma didn't talk about the subject, so I never felt I had a right to. It was our unintentional secret, I guess. The one I was still waiting for her to share.

I gave Maribel and Marilinda their tip from Mrs. Teagarden, and we went right back to wrapping. Momma was ringing up a line of folks at the checkout counter. Customers crowded the store's center aisle, some waiting for their gift wrap, some just for everyday hardware supplies.

"Here you go, Mr. Boudreaux." Momma handed a scrawny man two brown paper sacks full of nails. "A pound each, sixpenny and tenpenny. Raul is cutting your wire. You can pick it up around back."

"Ah sho' do thank ya much, Ms. Jeannie," Mr. Boudreaux said. He was a Louisiana-born Creole with olive skin and pitch-black eyes.

"His words come out smooth, like spreading warm butter on a hot roll," Maribel said softly as she taped up a package.

Mr. Boudreaux used words like *Naw'lins* for *New Orleans*. We loved to hear him talk.

Some of the customers stepped away from him; they scrolled their eyes from his dirty straw hat down to his rubber boots. He had a reputation for fighting roosters for money, cockfighting. Momma said folks just like to create myths out of people they don't understand, and all she knew for certain was that Lafitte Boudreaux's brown eggs made better omelets and richer pound cakes than any store-bought variety.

He dug his hand into his shirt pocket. "Lemme give a dollah ahn dis."

Momma stopped him. "Now, you keep your dollars in your pocket. You've got an account here, and I'll let you know when it's time to pay." Accounts were something else Supermart didn't have. Momma gave people accounts when they needed supplies but didn't have money. It wasn't charging because there was no credit card, no interest, and no payout plan. Country farmers like Mr. Boudreaux got the supplies they needed and paid what they could when they could. Mr. Boudreaux rarely paid in cash. Instead, he'd bring us fresh eggs and honey and even jars of gumbo.

"Wha's dis ah hear 'bout Miss Aus'in wahna chicken?"

"She's joining the Future Farmers of America, Mr. Boudreaux," Momma explained. "So she's taking up chicken fancy."

"I want to win the poultry contest at the fair," I added, tying a red yarn bow on another package.

"Ya sho' don' wahn no egg laya, then," he said. "Whasha needs a some pretty bird." Mr. Boudreaux turned to Momma. "Ms. Jeannie," he said, his words rolling like a deep, slow river, "come down ol 'Possum Trot in two, three day. Bring Miss Aus'in." Then he strolled away from the other customers' turned-up noses and downcast stares and left the

16

store humming and whistling, showing the snobs they had no power over him.

"BAM," Maribel said, slapping a candy-cane striped package on the counter. "You think he knows Chef Emeril?"

"Maribel watches the Food Network too much," Marilinda added.

I doubted Lafitte Boudreaux knew Chef Emeril Lagasse, but I was certain he knew something else: Lafitte Boudreaux knew poultry.

3
christmas eve blues

Momma didn't talk much on Christmas Eves, especially rainy ones.

Rain pelted the Jeep's canvas top as we pulled away from downtown Big Wells. The courthouse Christmas tree twinkled in silence, and the light-up, waving Santa Claus in the window of Wanda's Antique Mall stood dark and still.

We dropped Maribel and Marilinda off at their house just past the railroad tracks. Cars littered their front yard, and the girls had to zigzag around them to get to the porch. Lights were on all over their house, the curtains pulled wide. Through the windows, I could see Maribel's little cousins chasing each other. A man tuned a guitar in the living room, and a chubby girl danced in a circle with her hands clapping above her head. In the kitchen, Mamanita, Maribel's grandmother, stirred a big, steaming pot with one hand and pointed instructions with the other. They were having a real *feliz Navidad*.

Maribel's father scooted out the front door and down the steps, hustling in the rainy night around the oddly parked cars. I opened the Jeep door.

"Dolores made tamales." He smiled, handing us a warm foil-wrapped package. His forehead dripped with rain.

"Thank you," Momma and I sang together. "Merry Christmas."

Maribel and Marilinda were sure lucky, I thought.

Momma and I rode away in silence. She drove way past the turnoff to our house; her mind must've been somewhere else, because no one could miss our street. Delta could've landed a 747 on Camellia Heights. White Christmas lights lined the yards, like a residential, airport runway.

Momma's mind must've been on Daddy, so I just let her drive. It's not like it was the first time. Texas is truly a wide-open space with roads—paved and unpaved, red dirt and blacktop—spidering out from old downtown squares. Momma could just set out. Lose herself on the lost highways.

We were headed down Highway 37—miles outside of Big Wells—toward Prosper Lake. We passed Fortenberry Fruits; acres of leafless peach trees with bare-boned branches guarded the hills like a skeleton army. Rounding the curve, we sped by Farhat Farms, a white-fenced pasture with two red barns and its own roadside billboard:

FARHAT FARMS
Home of the Spotted Donkey
And
Reigning state champion barrel racer
TEXANNE FARHAT

"That girl even has her own billboard." I said it loud, trying to make conversation. Momma couldn't hear me. When the Jeep got above fifty miles per hour, the canvas top flapped loudly, like the big flag at the Ford dealership. Or maybe she didn't want to hear me. We were within a mile of Prosper Lake.

Momma flipped the blinker and slowed down in the middle of the highway just before Old Cypress Bridge. The rain had stopped, but fog puffed gray and smoky in the head-lights' beams.

She had a right to be alone with her thoughts, as she called it, and I hated to upset her with picky questions. This was a tough season for her to get through, but I just couldn't sit there and not say a word.

"Are we going back now?" I asked.

"Not a chance." Momma shifted gears, shot across the pavement, and took off on a one-lane, potholed excuse for a road.

She half scared me stiff. Since Daddy's death, Momma had treated Christmas Eves and rain-covered roads and Prosper Lake like an annual threat. She'd go all Rip Van Winkle on me and sleep through Christmas.

"Hang on!" I thought I saw her grin as I bounced white-knuckled around in the Jeep.

"Where are we?" I gripped the Jeep's roll bar with one hand as Momma swerved to miss crater-size puddles. I had never been this deep into the woods.

"Possum Trot." She drew a smile, ear to ear. "We've gotta get you a chicken."

About two miles off the highway, we slowed to a crawl in front of an antique gas station in a bend of the forgotten road: Possum Trot. Lafitte Boudreaux's neck of the woods.

"This bend is where Old Cypress Creek turns and feeds into Prosper Lake," she explained. "He's got creek bottom behind him, not too far from the bridge." Her voice faded on the bridge part, and she put both hands on the wheel. I could tell being this close to the lake in the rain on Christmas Eve was getting to her. No matter how big a smile she faked.

Momma pulled the Jeep off the blacktop and onto the gravel in front of the old gas pumps. A string of blue Christmas lights hung in swags around Lafitte Boudreaux's filling station home. We stepped out.

The two gas pumps, one with a flying red Pegasus that said MOBIL, rusted between rock columns.

"People used to drive under here." Momma stood under the porte cochere, a roofed pass-through connecting the gas pumps with the house.

"They obviously didn't have SUVs." I pointed up at the low roof.

I had heard stories for years about the old man living in the woods, fighting roosters for money and selling bootleg whiskey. I always imagined his operation to be more like a convenience store on Friday night. But there was none of that. The old gas station had a heavy weight about it. A sinking weight. Maybe it was the rock sides with the fog pressing against them. But between the blue lights and the dark night, I felt like I was being held underwater.

A discarded bait shop sign leaned against the rock wall of the house.

"I don't think he's here," I said. The screen door dangled from one hinge, and the wood door behind it looked like it hadn't been open for years.

"Shhhh." Momma put her finger in front of her lips. "Listen."

Momma and I stood perfectly still and silent in the wet, blue night. A man's voice, humming and deep, traded time with the roll of piano keys.

"Merry Christmas, baby," the voice bellowed between the piano's rocking ding-ding-a-dong. "Ain't no snow fallin' on the trees."

Momma patted my shoulder. "Go around back."

"Yeah, well, I think I'll just follow the leader." I got behind her. When I made up my mind that I would do whatever it took to be a hood ornament in next year's no-Jesus parade, I didn't have *Extreme Chicken Shopping* on the checklist. But if spending Christmas Eve in the boondocks in the rain got me a first-place chicken and a chance at showing up Dean Ottmer, then I'd take that round of compromise and risk.

Momma and I inched around the gas station house. "Don't get near the windows." She pointed to the two woodpaned windows. Through the blue of the Christmas lights, I could see shards of broken glass and broken bottles twinkling along the windowsills.

"That's one way to keep out robbers," I said.

"Not robbers," Momma corrected, "spirits. It's a voodoo practice to keep evil out." Why she had to throw out the word *voodoo* while we were sneaking around in the dark listening to an old man's moan is beyond me. I was spooked enough. The place reminded me of Daddy's bedtime fairy tales, redneck fairy tales, as he liked to call them. The ones where Prince Charmings wrestled alligators and little girl princesses pulled monster catfish from the creek with their bare hands.

Lafitte Boudreaux's property fell in a deep slope downward to the creek. A porchlike shack, built on stilts and jutting from the back of his filling station house, towered above us. It seemed to hang in the treetops. We edged along the rickety, wooden stilts.

"I bet he keeps a double-barrel shotgun propped up by a door," I whispered, remembering the gossip about his illegal rooster fights. The music stopped.

"Mr. Boudreaux!" Momma hollered up to the porch. Plastic covered the sides, and a light was on.

"Momma, honestly, do you think you should be yelling?" She didn't answer me; I was starting to think she'd finally come unhinged.

We were at least fifteen feet below the porch, knee-deep in dead weeds and damp from the last of the rain. "Mr. Boudreaux?" she tried again.

The light inside the porch spread to the treetops outside. It just floated in the darkness among the twisted branches like a mystic refuge. "He stays in a glowing, yellow tree house," I said.

I looked around. Possum Trot had taken us deep into the backwoods where giant cypress trees crowd together and hover over black water, as pallbearers hover over a coffin. Water moccasins hid around the creek banks and hung in trees, but it was too cold for them. Alligators would be out, though . . . so would coyotes and wild hogs. I took a few steps closer to Momma. When I moved, something or someone stepped behind me. My mind wasn't playing tricks on me either. Something was definitely behind me. Stalking me.

I inched a couple steps forward.

Then a couple more.

Mindful that I was being tracked, haunted by the fact that Mr. Boudreaux kept the evil spirits outside.

Hot breath steamed my lower back like a phantom spiriting up my spine.

I felt a pull, a tugging under my rain slicker. I stopped dead still. The tugging did not. I looked around for a bush; maybe I was just hung up on a limb. But I wasn't. Something had my shirt. Pulled me backwards.

"MOMMA!" I screamed, in a panic. The thing pulled me away from her. I screamed again and threw my arms around in the dark, fighting nothing but air.

"Hol' up, hol' up now." Lafitte Boudreaux's muddy river drawl cut into the night. He pushed me away with one hand

and yanked a rope around a goat with the other. They'd both snuck up out of nowhere. "He jus' wahn be somebody friend."

I jumped around in the knee-high grass, swatting air and twisting my shirttail tight around my waist.

"It's just a goat, Austin," Momma said, shaking her head. Her serious side had returned. "Just a goat."

I took a good look at the beast. Stark white face. Pointy beard. Upturned horns. The thing was a demon.

"We sho' wahn lookin' to creep up ahn ya," Mr. Boudreaux said. "Ah'd been watchin' for ya. Ah'd jus' stepped out to check my birds." He pointed down the back slope of his property. The moon had broken through the clouds. Dozens of tin-roofed chicken coops reflected its ghostly light.

"Miss Aus'in, sho' don' wahn no goat," he laughed, tying the devil to one of the wooden stilts. "But Ah sho' got summin' ya gahn like."

We followed Mr. Boudreaux up the narrow plank steps to his tree house porch.

I kept checking behind me for his possessed goat.

Inside, the room glowed from the single, yellow lightbulb hanging in the middle. He had a round table with four mismatched chairs, and a blanket-covered droopy sofa loaded with three cardboard boxes. An old upright piano was pushed against the back wall, and an electric guitar leaned in the corner. Faded concert posters, with names like James "Sugar Boy" Crawford and Guitar Slim, papered the ceiling.

25

"We heard you playing when we drove up," Momma said. "Mr. Boudreaux played blues with some of Louisiana's best back in the fifties," she explained.

"Ya momma ak'in' lak Ah's Champion Jack Dupree," he said. "Ah's jus' playin' swamp pop." Mr. Boudreaux picked up one of the boxes off the sofa and placed it on the table. "Miss Aus'in." He stuck both his hands in the box. "Dis called a Black-tail White Japanese hen." A fat white chicken with a pale pink beak and black tail feathers sat motionless in his arms. It looked like an old granny in a bad Easter hat. I tried to smile.

"Ya ain't takin' no shine to this'un, Ah see." He put the thing back in its box.

Momma jabbed her finger in my back. "I'm grateful for any chicken, Mr. Boudreaux," I quickly said. "But I was hoping for one with more color."

Mr. Boudreaux laughed and put another box on the table. "Dis a Mottle Japanese pullet." He pulled out a black-and-white spotted bird.

"It's the Dalmatian of chickens," Momma said. I liked it until she said that. But Dean Ottmer's voice started hammering in my head. "Austin Gray crossbred a dog with a chicken and this is what she got. That thing's as weird-looking as she is."

"You got anything without spots?" I asked, hoping not to get another jab.

Mr. Boudreaux switched boxes again and sang, "Say

26

what ya mean and mean what ya say. Ol' Lafitte won't get confused dat way."

Momma grinned, a real grin, so I knew I was in the clear.

"Now, Ah ain' fixin' to wake this'un up." He put the last box on the table. "Dis a some pretty bird, but he sassy."

I looked into the box. The chicken had fluffy plumes so shiny black they looked midnight blue.

"This a Black Rosecomb Bantam." Mr. Boudreaux added, "He a Bantam rooster."

"The fair has a poultry category for Bantams," I said. I really wanted to ask if it was one of his fighting roosters, but I'd just be giving lip to the local rumor mill. Momma hated that. She spent the first year after Daddy's death trying to clear up the rumor about him being drunk that night. Finally, one customer too many came in the store and asked her about it. She threw up her hands and said, "Believe what you want to believe, but don't come in here poking me with a stick anymore." Word travels fast in Big Wells. No one has mentioned anything about Daddy being drunk since. To our faces, at least.

Mr. Boudreaux drew his finger across the red spikes on top of the rooster's head. "This a right perfect comb," he said. "Some flop over, this'un stand straight up. He small, maybe weigh a pound and a half. Ya can hol' him in one hand. But he a little aristocrat. Come daytime, he strut aroun' ches' out tellin' the world whatta do."

Momma stood by the door with her hands in her back pockets.

"This is the one." I smiled.

"Well, Mr. Boudreaux"—Momma pulled a folded stack of bills from her pocket—"I guess we owe you for a . . ." She paused. "What did you call him?"

"He a Black Rosecomb Bantam, and he gahna be hard to beat in that fair." He put his right hand up and waved Momma off. "Put ya dollahs up. You's on account."

Mr. Boudreaux gave us a bucket full of slugs and a sack of something called blood meal. He said it would keep the rooster's feathers silky. He told us to put Vaseline on the comb, that red spiky thing on its head. Mr. Boudreaux said Vaseline would keep the comb from getting damaged from frostbite.

Before we left, Momma got Mr. Boudreaux to play swamp pop boogie-woogie on the piano. We clapped along, and he'd throw his head back and holler out a song. When he realized we hadn't eaten supper, he brought out two re-cycled Cool Whip containers filled with hot rice and steamy crawfish etouffee. He picked some on his guitar while Momma and I ate. It was our best Christmas Eve in a long time, and I felt almost as lucky as Maribel. Momma still didn't say much, but she seemed to forget for a time the rain and the season and the night Daddy drowned.

charles dickens and his christmas carol

"er—EERR, ER—A—EERR!"

Other than taking down the decorations at Gray's True Value, Momma and I have had one Christmas Day tradition for the last few years: We sleep late, sometimes until noon.

I rolled over and slapped my alarm clock even though it hadn't gone off.

5:27 A.M.

"er—EERR, ER—A—EERR!"

Momma opened my bedroom door. She wore a long, oversized T-shirt that had BAH-HUMBUG spelled out on the front. She resurrected that thing every December since Daddy's death and looked as unhappy as its message. "Austin, your new responsibility is wishing you a Merry Christmas."

The rooster. I hopped out of bed and took off down the hall. Momma and I had put him in his box in the laundry room. We didn't have a coop yet, so we couldn't leave him outside.

"er—EERR, ER—A—ERRR!"

The rooster sat on a stack of books decorating the fireplace mantel: *Great Expectations, David Copperfield, A Tale of Two Cities, A Christmas Carol.*

"I must've left the laundry room door open," I said.

Perched on top of *A Christmas Carol,* the rooster acted like he had written it, and it was his to tell. He stuck his coal-black chest out and belted out another round, "er—EERR, ER—A—ERRR!" Then he skittered about four side steps off the book and fanned both wings downward, out, and up—his very own performance finale.

"Looks like Charles Dickens has been reincarnated as your FFA project," Momma said.

I tiptoed toward the fireplace. He was a fancy bird, as fancy as the iron rooster weather vane on top of Texanne Farhat's red barn. Seeing him for the first time in good light, I felt my odds of becoming the FFA Sweetheart had just improved. He was a plump, black mass of feathers with a bright red crown sitting on his head like a top hat. Except for his greenish eyes darting around the room, he looked stuffed. He proudly turned his head left to right, showing off the large, white lobes on each side. His long neck curved into his back, like a steep drop on a roller coaster. Then, just as steep, his tail feathers fanned up, only to drop again in long, sweeping plumes. I went for him with both hands.

"er—EERRRR!" he crowed, flying to the other side of the mantel.

The rooster knocked over Momma's autographed picture of Matthew McConaughey, which the actor had personally given her when he passed through town and needed a new hinge for the screen door of his trailer. He came in the store shirtless, and Momma tripped over herself getting him a pack of hinges.

"Austin, remember you have to grab the rooster by his legs," Momma said.

I wasn't sure about grabbing his legs. Roosters had spurs, sharp bony projections on each leg they used as weapons. Mr. Boudreaux had hand-raised him, so I didn't think he'd spur me. But the rooster had to learn to trust us. Mr. Boudreaux told us definitely not to grab his wings until then.

I eased closer to him, slipping my hand under his belly, palm up. His nubby shanks stiffened like little twigs as I grasped his legs between my fingers. I gently picked him up off the mantel, pulled him to my stomach, and cradled him. The rooster's silky tail feathers draped over my arm.

"There, boy," I said. His belly was warm, and his heart beat in my palm.

"There's nothing *boy* about that rooster," Momma said, repositioning Matthew McConaughey. "He's the boss cock in this house and he knows it." She walked into the kitchen, put on her glasses, dropped a couple scoops of coffee in the pot, and peeled the plastic wrap off a loaf of pumpkin bread someone had given us. She smiled at me. "We're just a couple of broody hens he thinks he can supervise."

"What should I name him?" He seemed content to stay

in my arms, so I scooted a bar stool out with my foot and sat at the kitchen counter with Momma.

"Something appropriate for a bossy little man: Napoleon, John McEnroe, Tom Cruise."

The rooster puffed up and crowed, "HAAAWK!" I let both arms go and he flew back to the mantel, right on top of the collected works of Charles Dickens.

"Well, he's not so fond of your suggestions," I said.

"You better hope he doesn't poop on those books."

The rooster again perched on top of *A Christmas Carol*. "He seems to like Dickens," Momma said. "Why don't you call him Scrooge or Pickwick or Pip?"

He wasn't old like Scrooge, and Pip sounded too much like Pipsqueak. I wanted him to have an important name, not something Dean Ottmer could easily make fun of. Even better, I wanted a name Dean Ottmer couldn't even understand.

The rooster flew down to the fireplace hearth and paced back and forth, clucking some and flapping his wings. He had an arrogant little strut: a chest-out, beak-up, tail-feather bounce that commanded attention. With his long neck, scooped-out back, and peacocklike backside, he looked like a fluffy, black Victorian teapot. Even though she kept her arms folded and smirked, Momma couldn't keep her eyes off him either.

"The judges give points for personality, don't they?" she said, pouring coffee into two Santa Claus mugs.

"Personality *and* stage presence," I added. The rooster

32

looked back at me and flaunted his swagger. "He can sure put on a show. . . . Charles Dickens," I announced.

"What about him?" Momma said. She squeezed chocolate syrup into my mug. "Here's your Christmas mocha." We clanked our mugs together, and she gave me her best Merry Christmas kiss on the top of my head.

"Charles Dickens," I continued. "Our English teacher said last year that Charles Dickens read his books in public." I stirred my mocha. "People came in droves to hear him. That's what's going to happen when *he* takes the stage." I pointed my spoon at the rooster. "He's gonna light it up."

My plan to become a hood ornament just shifted into fifth gear. "Momma, we're looking at Charles Dickens, the blue-ribbon winner of next year's Prosper County Fair, Poultry Division."

Charles Dickens flew over by Momma's plate of sliced pumpkin bread. He scraped at it with his slate-blue claws, then pecked and nibbled a few bites.

"Mrs. Cratchit," Momma said to me. "I think Charles Dickens needs his own Christmas pudding." She held her Santa Claus mug with both hands and blew across the top of the coffee. "He probably needs a potty break, too. I don't want chicken droppings in my house."

I carried Charles Dickens into the backyard. The sun was up and bright, and Big Wells was in for another yellow Christmas: no snow, just sunlight. Mr. Boudreaux said Bantams like fresh air and sunshine, and the rooster seemed frisky as he pecked around in the brown grass. I pulled on one of Momma's garden gloves and grabbed a couple of slugs from the bucket Mr. Boudreaux sent. I placed them, slimy and wriggling, on the ground. Charles Dickens stuck his long neck out, snatched one up, and took off. He waddled side to side and bobbed his head when he ran, his own happy dance. I laughed out loud. "Charles Dickens, you funky chicken!" I must've insulted him because he stopped, swung his red-combed head in my direction, and crowed, "HAAAWK." Despite his protest, I still felt like he was a trophy-winning attraction. When he stood like a statue and the wind blew through his raven-colored feathers, he looked too pretty to be real. But he was real, real with lots of attitude. Together, Charles Dickens and I were going to make Prosper County Fair history.

Momma said he'd be just fine inside the back fence, so we left him outside while we exchanged our Christmas gifts. I'm the only child of only children, and I'm down to one parent. Gift exchanges never take long. I had a FedExed present from my daddy's mother and my sole living grandparent: Glammy, the self-described glamorous grandmother. She moved to Florida with her sister after my grandfather died and before I started school. She came back once, and that was for Daddy's funeral. Momma said she was never the small-town type.

I opened the FedEx package. Two small, white envelopes fell out: one addressed to me, one to Momma. "I wonder what ailment she's got that prevented her from coming this year," I said. "A cruise? An African safari? Tea with the queen?"

"Your Glammy is who she is. If she tried to be like, say, Maribel's grandmother, she'd fail miserably." Momma opened her envelope. "*Sweet Jeannie,*" Momma read aloud. "*What a whirlwind this year has been! Sister and I have seen the Great Wall in China. We even took a ride in a rickshaw. We're back, but we've taken up ballroom dancing. I'm hard at work on my samba. Enjoy the purse. It's made in China. I brought it back special for you. Love, Dinah.*" Momma pulled two tiny silk purses from the FedEx package.

"That might hold your cell phone," I said. "Or my lip gloss." I opened my envelope. "*Sweet Austin.*" I ratcheted my voice up a couple notches. "*What a whirlwind year this has been! Sister and I have seen the Great Wall in China. We even took a ride in a rickshaw. We're back, but we've taken up ballroom dancing. I'm hard at work on my samba. Enjoy the purse. It's made in China. I brought it back special for you. Love, Glammy.*" Momma and I hung the pocket purses over our shoulders and laughed. "Sister," I said to Momma in my high voice. "Let's go for a rickshaw ride." We laughed and laughed.

Charles Dickens must've felt left out. He flew onto the kitchen windowsill and crowed right along with us.

I gave Momma her present, a downloaded CD of seventies music that I made myself.

"I love it," she said. I could tell she really did. "Fleetwood Mac, ELO, Boston. We'll play these on the way to the store this afternoon." She handed me a box wrapped in Gray's True Value candy-cane striped paper.

"HAAAAAWK! HAAAAWK!" Charles Dickens was wound up on the patio.

"I thought Charles Dickens was my present," I said, tearing off the paper. I lifted the lid off the box. Inside was a purple-and-black check skullcap and scarf to match.

"I know that violates my rule against wasting money on winter clothes," she said. Momma never bought more than a rain-resistant jacket because this part of East Texas rarely gets that cold. "But you're going to be taking care of that rooster outside, and those should keep you from freezing to death. Besides, the purple and black will be pretty with your dark hair." Her voice softened. She rubbed her fingers across the soft wool scarf. "Your daddy used to wear a purple tie with black stripes. He always looked so handsome."

"HAAAAWK, HAAAAWK!"

Momma jerked her hand back like she'd touched something hot. "That rooster cannot do that all day, Austin," she snapped. "The neighbors will vote us off the island."

"He's just caroling." Then I remembered Mr. Boudreaux's warning. Crowing and clucking is just normal rooster chatter. But if he crows anything that sounds like the word *hawk*, the rooster is either ticked off or in trouble.

I looked to the kitchen window where Charles Dickens had been perched and squawking. A black feather floated past the panes. Charles Dickens was gone. In his place, crouched and twitchy, sat our next-door neighbor's free-roaming, bird-mauling cat.

marauders

"Get outta here, WhizBang!" Momma clapped her hands and charged the cat.

WhizBang darted about twenty feet, stopped, and pinned his eyes on her. A blue Siamese, he was the color of steel. "Get outta here, I said." Momma stomped her foot twice, and WhizBang jumped onto the fence. He wanted to pounce — staring us down, flicking his tail.

"GO!" I threw a rock at him. "You stupid cat."

WhizBang disappeared over the fence. Charles Dickens was nowhere in sight. Just a few black feathers whirling in the Christmas wind.

"He couldn't have eaten him, right?" I pulled out a long, sickle-like feather stuck in the screen door. Doomed. I was sure it was written in the FFA manual somewhere that the sweetheart had to keep her livestock alive.

"There's no blood." Momma looked under the windowsill and across the backyard. "WhizBang didn't swipe anything but feathers. Charles Dickens got spooked." She blocked the sun with her hand and looked toward the roof. "Chickens can't fly that far or that high. He's probably hiding."

Momma and I circled our house, looking to the roof and in the trees. No Charles Dickens. Standing on the sidewalk, we scanned the street. Camellia Heights was a historic neighborhood, dead-ending in a grand English Tudor. The brick and rock houses leading up to it, all built around the 1920s, had arched entrances and steep, pointy roofs with tall chimneys. The front yards were deep and shaded by hulking oaks. Too many places for a rooster to hide.

A group crowded together up the street: Dean Ottmer, his older brother, and nearby boys they bullied into their clique. Unfortunately, the Ottmers lived in our neighborhood. They'd blown into town five years ago and bought everything important—the Ford dealership and Judge Martin's ivy-covered mansion anchoring the end of Camellia Heights. The Ottmer boys were probably showing off their Santa Claus booty: paintball guns, hunting rifles, remote-controlled this and that, designer jeans, the latest basketball shoes.

"Austin"—Momma pulled her hands to her hips—"go back to the house." That was her answer for everything. Shelter Austin. She stepped in front of me, trying to block my view of the Ottmer gang. But I was taller than she was. Something buzzed behind her.

"HAAAWK, HAAAWK!"

A remote-controlled toy Hummer raced after Charles Dickens, chasing him. He ran in mad circles, flying a few feet and flapping his wings. The Hummer stayed hot on his tail feathers. Charles Dickens scurried to get out of the road. He could fly onto a tree if he could make it to a yard. But the Hummer cut him off every time he neared the curb. The boys hooted and howled; that is, until they saw Momma. Dean handed off the controls and snatched Charles Dickens with both hands.

That was it. I thought I'd blow up all big and green like the Hulk.

"Go home, Austin," Momma said. "I'll take care of this."

The boys, five or six maybe, banded together. In the middle, as usual, stood Dean Ottmer . . . with both hands squeezed around my chicken.

"PUT HIM DOWN!" I screamed and ran toward them. Dean Ottmer had no respect for life. I had seen him randomly popping birds and squirrels with a pellet gun in his own front yard. No doubt he'd torture my rooster to exhaustion.

Momma took off after me. She jogged every day, so she wasn't far behind.

Dean Ottmer tucked Charles Dickens under his arm like he was carrying a football. "Haawk!" Charles Dickens tried to crow, but it sounded weak as if it were his last cry for help. Some of the boys folded their arms. Dean Ottmer's brother, Sammy, the one who failed the drug pee test in football, stepped forward. He wore a T-shirt so new that the creases from being folded showed. It had I ♥ HOT MOMS emblazoned on the front. "What do you want, Austin?" He acted like WhizBang did on top of the fence, like he wanted to pounce. His eyes shifted from me to Momma. He blew out a long whistle. "Are you"—Sammy looked Momma up and down—"and your mom wanting to play?"

Their sleazy hangers-on hummed a collective "*Ooooooooo.*" The Ottmer boys had no respect for women, no matter what the age.

"Give him to me, Dean." My ears were ringing. I wanted to punch him and his freak brother.

"I just don't see a collar with your name on it." Dean had on a new camouflage jacket with the tags still attached at the wrist—a mistake I'm sure he'd fix after everyone knew the price. Charles Dickens's blue legs dangled under Dean's camo coat. Black feathers drooped over his arms. The rooster struggled—trying to extend his head and neck and trying to free himself.

"You're smashing his wings," I said through my teeth.

"Here." Momma reached out and took Charles Dickens from Dean Ottmer's clutches. She didn't ask. He didn't argue. "If he gets out again, you know where we live." I took Charles Dickens from her; his heart pounded in my palm.

"Whatcha get, Austin?" Dean jabbed. "A chicken for Christmas?" His gang fell out like it was the funniest thing they'd ever heard Dean say.

We turned our backs on the boys, their whispers, then their laughter.

"They're talking about us," I said as we walked home.

"You care?"

40

"No," I lied. I didn't want to care, but I did. Even though I despised him and I'd love to run his sorry butt down in a Hummer like he did to Charles Dickens, I just couldn't get out from under Dean Ottmer's smothering insults and constant harassment. I didn't need for him to like me; I just needed for him to shut up. *Chestless, Stork, AuSTINK*. What other people say is not supposed to matter, but the truth is, it does. Dean Ottmer's insults mattered. There. I said it. They mattered because there was enough truth to make my classmates, sometimes even the teachers, laugh—like when Coach Watson told us in history about infrastructure. He explained road construction using Interstate 30 as an example. "It's just one flat stretch of road," he said. Dean added, "Like Austin Gray. No hills and no curves." Everyone thought Dean Ottmer was funny. Everyone but those of us in his comedy routine.

By the time we got back to our house, Charles Dickens's heartbeat slowed. He seemed quiet. I put him down, but he didn't move off the patio.

"He's looking for WhizBang," Momma said.

"Or Dean Ottmer," I added.

She brought out a bowl of water and a baggie full of salad. "Put this out."

I sprinkled the salad on the grass right next to the patio. Charles Dickens didn't touch it. He took a couple side steps, then flew onto the back of Momma's glider. I picked up the slug bucket, reached in with two fingers, and pinched a fat one.

41

"Here you go, Charles Dickens." I dropped the slug on top of the lettuce mound. "Slug Salad."

He sailed down from his perch on the glider and pecked at the slug. He didn't skitter away with it. He didn't run around in a happy dance either. WhizBang and Dean Ottmer had caused him to hesitate and stay close in. I knew exactly how he felt.

Momma came out with my new cap and scarf and Charles Dickens's box. "We've got to take down the Christmas decorations at the store." She looked at the rooster's downturned wings and heavy eyes. "We better take him with us."

In the Jeep, Charles Dickens didn't stay in his box. Instead, he perched on the top of the backseat. Momma tried not to stress him anymore, so she drove slowly, carefully crossing the railroad tracks by Maribel's house. Maribel and her family visited her cousins on Christmas Day, and her usually car-covered front yard was empty now. Farther up the street, a discarded blue spruce lay alone on the curb. The jumbo, inflatable this-n-thats—snow globes, Frosties, Santas—normally lit up and puffed up were nothing more than withered plastic heaps of has-been yard art. Since Daddy's death, Christmas always felt like an ending to me: a day to take down, clean out, put away.

Momma pulled around the downtown square and parked in front of Gray's True Value. Not a soul in sight, just Mayor Nesmith's gold Mercedes parked illegally in a handicap spot in front of the courthouse steps.

"Hurry and get in the store before he sees us," Momma said.

In addition to his swanky ride, Mayor Nesmith had a money-blowing wife, four whiny rugrats, and the hots for my momma. She avoided him like poison ivy.

Once inside, I put Charles Dickens down on the wood floor. He waddled around an empty work-glove display that had been picked over by last-minute shoppers. He clucked once and skittered around the garden section at the front of the store. Momma had a pegboard with rakes and hoes and shovels hanging from hooks. She took one of the rakes, turned it sideways, and hung it horizontally across the peg board. Charles Dickens landed on his new perch. His red wattle jiggled. His blue claws grasped the rake's handle. He blinked his eyes.

"He likes it there," I said. He could see out both front windows, and he was near Momma and me. He watched us box the decorations.

Every Christmas since I was two, the window of Gray's True Value was home to a snowman family. It was as much a Big Wells tradition as the Christmas parade. The daddy snowman pulled a Gray's True Value red wagon with a little snowgirl in it. The snowmomma held a sign: A JOYOUS SEASON FROM OUR FAMILY TO YOURS. But the season was over. Momma rolled up the white netting around the family. She swept up the fake snow, not saying a word. The steady swish-swish of her broom irritated the silence. I slipped trash bags over snowdaddy, snowgirl, and snowmomma.

I carried each, one at a time, to the decorations closet in the back of the store. I did it so Momma wouldn't have to. For her, putting away the snow family was like burying Daddy all over again, burying what was supposed to be our family.

Coming back down the center aisle, I stopped cold.

Mayor Nesmith, on the prowl, was standing in the garden section holding a campaign poster and chatting up my momma. His hair was steel gray, and he reminded me of WhizBang with his eyes pinned on her.

I hightailed it.

"Hey, gorgeous." He shifted my way as I closed in. "I haven't seen you in ages." Nesmith lied right through his bleach-white smile.

How about the Christmas parade? How about that greasy popcorn bag you shoved at me? I kept my questions to myself. Momma knew what a liar he was. No need for me to point out the obvious. I reached between them and lifted the Gray's True Value red wagon.

"Angel, let me help you with that." Nesmith went for one end of the wagon. The backs of his hands were hairy, silver and black nests.

"No." I jerked Daddy's wagon back.

Charles Dickens sailed off his rake perch. He plunged like a black torpedo toward Nesmith and his end of the wagon. "What the hell!" Nesmith jumped back. He threw the poster over his shoulder and into the plumbing section, right on top of the toilet flush valves. Charles Dickens landed on the wagon's handle, grasping it with one claw and hold-ing the other claw up at Mayor Nesmith.

"Victor." Momma inventoried the mess of flush valves and clenched her fists when she said his name. "Meet Charles Dickens. Austin's FFA project and, it looks like, our new resident rooster in charge." Momma slipped her hand under Charles Dickens, picked him up, and put him back on the rake. "I'm surprised he's so protec-tive." She stroked his wattle. "Maybe he just doesn't like males."

"Maybe he's just a good judge of character," I mumbled.

"That thing's real?" Nesmith dusted himself off but kept his distance. "I mean, I saw it perched over there with the garden stuff. I didn't think it was real. I thought it was just decoration." He ran his chubby fingers through his hair, then picked up his campaign sign.

"You shouldn't always assume pretty things to be *just dec-oration*." Momma turned his words on him. She always said Nesmith had a low opinion of women, otherwise he wouldn't tomcat around town right under his wife's nose.

"So, Jeannie, are you going to put my campaign sign in the window or not?" Nesmith changed the subject, keeping one eye on Charles Dickens.

"I have customers on both sides of the tracks," she ex-plained. "I'm in the hardware and gifts business. I'm not in the business of politics." She went back to sweeping.

"I know the last few years have been hard." Nesmith reached out to touch her.

I dropped the wagon onto the wood floor. The whole building rattled.

"Time to go, Victor." Momma pointed her broom handle at the door.

"Jeannie." Nesmith showed his teeth again. "This is an old building. Probably full of asbestos. I'd hate to see it condemned by some city inspector." Nesmith reached his hairy hand toward Momma. "You have options, Jeannie Gray." Charles Dickens popped his wings out like a Japanese fan. Nesmith pulled his hand back and slid it into his pocket. "You should consider all of them when choosing how you plan to support me."

"Your bullying's not working, Victor." Momma stepped toward Nesmith. He picked the wrong season to mess with her. "Don't make the mistake of overlooking a couple of very real things. Gray's True Value isn't a building, it's a landmark." She tapped her broom on the front door. "That marker on the outside is from the TEXAS state historical society, Victor, not the city of Big Wells. Send your inspection report to them."

Nesmith tried staring at her boobs. When Dean Ottmer did that to girls, they got nervous and couldn't focus on what they were saying. But Momma didn't miss a beat. "Furthermore, this building isn't the business. *I'm* the business." His intimidation had failed, so he looked her in the face. She eyeballed him. "My customers go where I go. For that reason alone, I don't take political sides."

Mayor Nesmith grinned. "Well, thank you for supporting me by not supporting anyone." He opened the door and frowned at Charles Dickens. "I'll even ignore the city ordinance against farm animals as pets."

"Oh, and, Victor?" Momma turned her back to me like she didn't want me to hear. She pointed the broom handle at Nesmith's nose. "I'm not one bit interested in you, so stop the candy-coated hints. Don't make that mistake again, especially in front of my daughter."

Mayor Nesmith laughed. I don't think he took her seriously. He went on down the block, putting his sign in someone else's storefront.

"He's the devil," I said.

"Only if you let him be." Momma cleaned the spray snow off the window. "Everyone has an adversary. They either break you or make you better." She handed me a box of paper snowflakes. "It seems as though you have Dean Ottmer. Charles Dickens, there . . ." She pointed at him. "Looks like he's got WhizBang."

"By next Christmas," I said, "I intend to shut the Deandevil up for good."

"I hope that works out for you." She put her arm around my shoulder. "But if putting on pretty dresses and riding off on sporty cars silenced the Dean Ottmers of the world, we'd all be hood ornaments in the No-Jesus Christmas Parade."

"It's a start," I said.

"Yes, but it'd be a lot less work to just tell him to stick it."

I thought about that, about telling *Dean-O* to stick it. I thought about it all the way home . . . past every closed fast-food joint, past every dead Christmas tree, every pile of curbed Christmas garbage, every forgotten swag of Christmas lights. I thought about telling Dean Ottmer to stick it: up his nose, in his ear, where the sun don't shine. Ignoring his crap hadn't gotten me anywhere. By the time we neared the stuffed-Hefty-bag-and-empty-TV-box-lined Camellia Heights, I decided I wanted the pleasure of both—telling Dean off and being parade royalty.

"Out with the old, in with the new," I told Momma and Charles Dickens. "Next chance I get, I'm telling Dean-O to stick it."

Momma didn't turn into our driveway. She pulled in front and then backed crossways into the street, shining the Jeep's lights on our house.

"That chance may come around sooner than you realize."

Wound around the trees, rolled over the roof's pitch, and wrapped across our front porch, toilet paper covered the house in long, white strips.

6
stunt devil sticks it

Wrapping houses was Dean Ottmer's signature stunt. He even left a calling card—a giant, toilet paper *O* centered in the front yard.

Being in the same neighborhood, I was way too convenient. He wrapped our house four more times that winter: New Year's Eve, Presidents' weekend, Martin Luther King Jr. Day, one Teacher In-Service day. All the high-tech video games and weaponry couldn't keep him occupied for an extended school break.

He wore me flat out, but not my momma.

"Only an idiot toilet-papers the home of a hardware store owner." Momma repeated that every time Dean pulled his stunt. She was a before-dawn riser, and she owned power tools. Dean's toilet paper wrap job never once saw the light of day. He probably hadn't gotten settled back at his house good before Momma had a power washer out, shooting water into the trees and onto the roof. The soaked toilet paper fell to the ground, clumping and deteriorating. I raked it, bagged it, and put it on the curb—all before the sun came up.

"You know, Momma." I raked in the dark. "We could just call his parents or the police like everyone else in town does when he wraps them."

"What? And miss pissing Dean off?" Momma grinned as she shot a stream of water into the trees. "Besides, his parents don't hold him accountable for anything. They'll just send a cleanup crew, which, as you and I both know, is Sanchez Lawn Service. I'm not about to allow Maribel's father to clean up Dean's mess. And the police all work security part-time at Ottmer Ford." She gripped the spray gun like Rambo, firing water at the strips of toilet paper. "I'll take care of Dean."

After breakfast, Momma and I spotted Dean and his goons standing on the sidewalk in front of our house. He had come to show off his handiwork, but there was nothing to see. He kicked the trash bag on the curb three or four times; then they all skulked back up the street.

Momma laughed, like had-trouble-sipping-her-coffee laugh. She got some kind of pleasure out of ruining Dean's toilet paper terrorism. I really didn't care so much about the toilet paper. Dean's pranks could always get worse, vicious. I had an uneasy feeling that spoiling his wrap jobs was like pouring gas on a campfire. And I didn't want to be engulfed in a Dean-O bonfire.

At school, Dean was fairly easy to avoid. I had Pre-AP classes; he didn't. Dean ate lunch in the cafeteria with his brother and the football team. Maribel and I ate outside.

Dean hadn't toilet-papered our house in weeks. He was even out of town the whole week of spring break. I saw so little of him that I forgot at times about purposefully staying off his radar. But at school the week after spring break, I paid big-time for that memory lapse.

Maribel and I ate lunch every day in the Big Wells High courtyard—a parklike place between the cafeteria and the main school building. There were a couple of benches and picnic tables.

Maribel and I were sitting on a bench when a flying jalapeño slice landed in her black hair. Some jerk-off, bored with his nachos, decided it'd be a real hoot to pelt the Mexican girl with jalapeños. Genius.

Maribel pinched the pepper slice between her fingers, flicking it onto the ground. She squeezed the gooey cheese out of her hair.

They should've stopped with the flying pepper. But no.

Some boy from a loud line of wall-leaners shouted, "Jalapeño! Jalapeño *chica*!"

I slid to the edge of the bench, giving Maribel some room. She'd take the pepper wisecrack personally because that's how they intended it. Like most Mexican immigrants in town, her family came from the state of Puebla, so she was Poblano. Calling Maribel out in any way related to her culture was like poking a skunk.

Maribel faced her heckler with her fist in the air like she was leading the Cinco de Mayo charge for General Ignacio Zaragoza. "*Soy Poblana!*"

On the opposite side of the courtyard, a different gang — Hispanic boys in white T-shirts and saggy khaki pants — clustered together like metal beads on a magnet when they heard Maribel yell. I thought all hell was about to break loose.

"*Soy Poblana,*" she repeated, measuring the weight of her backup. Maribel deepened her voice to a careful warning: "Get your peppers right."

Then she sat down like nothing had happened and started eating her torta. The harassment over.

The Hispanic gang stared down the wall-leaners, who quickly turned away.

It was nothing new, but I always felt embarrassed when small-minded kids made stupid immigrant jokes. Like they never stopped to think how Anglos got here. I didn't know what else to say, so I apologized. "I'm sorry, Maribel."

Maribel stopped chewing. She swallowed hard, then smiled. "Don't be sorry for me, Austin. Be sorry for them. They have no awareness of the world around them, and it will catch up. Mamanita always says, *Camarón que se duerme se lo lleva lo corriente.*"

"Which means?"

"Shrimp that fall asleep get swept away by the current." Then she pointed across the courtyard to the Hispanic kids huddled together. "Let them call us Ancho, Habanero, Jalapeño — I don't care. Puebla was full of farmers, revolutionaries, strong Mexicans. That's my heritage. I feel sorry for those who don't know their own history and pay no attention to their present."

52

Maribel amazed me. Insults seemed to make her stronger—not a built-up, in-your-face bitterness, but more of a gathering resolve.

The lunchtime crowd seemed unconcerned with Maribel's personal history conviction. The band kids bunched together, including the tuba player, Lewis Fortenberry. He actually carried an Elvis lunch pail and was drinking from a thermos.

There really must be something to that safety-in-numbers thing.

I counted six other groups in the self-segregated courtyard: the wall-leaners with their massive egos and small minds, the Hispanics, the Goths with their black fingernails and studded belts, a few dance-team high kickers practicing their routines, the skaters in their skinny pencil-leg jeans, and the FFA.

FFA students hung around the courtyard in their member's-only cobalt blue corduroy jackets and their boots. Sundi Knutt, last year's parade sweetheart, was there. I watched her every move.

"She doesn't have her own jacket, Maribel. Watch." I noted a few other items of interest. Sundi completely filled out her jeans, and the faux pearl snaps on her shirt holding in her *girls*, as Momma called them, looked ready to pop. Every day, cold or not, Sundi rubbed the tops of her arms and hopped up and down until one of the boys gave up his FFA jacket, which never took long. She showed her appreciation by wrapping both arms around the waist of the now jacketless boy, keeping him warm.

"I'm buying my own coat," I told Maribel. No way could I pull off Sundi's jacket game. I got hives just thinking about it. Sundi pressed herself freely against everyone. She made being affectionate look natural, comfortable. For her, it seemed effortless. I suppose it helped to have brothers. But Sundi also had a daddy. Maybe that's why I get so jittery around boys; I haven't had anyone to practice on.

"She's a marshmallow girl." Maribel finished off the last of her torta.

"A marshmallow girl?"

"Sundi's a marshmallow," Maribel explained. "She's pudgy and squishy, soft with no hard edges. Other people are more like carrot sticks." Maribel looked at me. "They can be hard and snap."

"I do not snap." I tied my scarf around my neck and folded my arms. "When have I ever snapped?"

"Did I say I was talking about you? No," Maribel answered herself. "I was just saying Sundi's a marshmallow. That's all."

Sundi Knutt let go of jacket-boy and glanced our way.

"She heard you," I said through my teeth.

Sundi jogged toward us. She wrapped the jacket tight around her, keeping her girls from bouncing out of control. Half running, half shuffling, Sundi moved like it was blustery and cold, but it was spring—sunny and sixty degrees.

"Hey-ey." She stopped in front of our bench. "Scoot over." She wedged her plump butt between Maribel and me.

From a distance, Sundi looked like Marilyn Monroe. Up close, she was more like Norma Jean—still beautiful, just more real. "I hear you signed up for FFA next year. Daddy went to Gray's True Value. He said you had a Bantam cock that looked as good as any he's seen."

"That's Charles Dickens." I had never really talked to Sundi before. She was a year ahead of me in school, and it didn't count that she said "Hey" to everyone. Sundi had baby-blue eyes the size of quarters, and she wore blue mascara the color of the FFA jacket. I wondered if she had some county fair secret to share or some insider sweetheart knowledge that could help me. I tried giving her an opening. "He hates his coop," I offered. "So Momma takes him to the store. People stop in just to see him. I want him to like being handled; I'm entering him in the county fair."

"Cooool," she said, smiling. "I'm entering a lamb this year. She's snow white with a black face and feet. I bottle-fed her for six months." Sundi's heart shined in her blue eyes. "She's a pet, like your Charles Dickens."

Some of the boys from the FFA group must've missed Sundi because they walked toward us. "Hey-ey," she sang in two syllables to the boys. "Austin's entering a Bantam in the fair."

"What kind?" Josh Whatley asked. Sundi had ridden on the hood of his daddy's Ford in the parade. He was hot and parade-connected. Now he was talking to me. I thought I'd pee on myself.

"A Black Rosecomb." I tied my scarf again, and again.

"Austin feeds it homemade scratch," Maribel added. She could talk to the president and not get nervous.

"You make it yourself?" Josh asked. He had broad shoulders with chiseled arms. I'd seen him unloading bails of hay last summer, shirtless and sun-kissed.

"Lafitte Boudreaux makes it. He uses whole grains, not corn."

"Shoot, girl," one of the boys spit. "Is that one of that old man's fighting roosters?"

"No," I snapped. "It's my show bird. I've had him since Christmas."

Maribel raised an eyebrow at me and folded her arms. I could tell she thought I was a carrot.

The school bell rang. Sundi reached both arms up, and Josh Whatley took her hands and pulled her off the bench. "Later, ladies." She smiled and bounced off.

Josh Whatley turned around. "I can bring you some slugs if you need them." He kept his thin lips closed when he smiled. "Chickens need the protein. They love slugs."

"They do-do love slugs," I stuttered. Josh pushed his bangs out of his face, grinned shyly, and faded into the students heading into the building.

Maribel and I watched him walk.

As sudden as a shotgun blast, Dean Ottmer jumped onto the bench where Maribel and I had been sitting.

"They do-do! They do-do!" He flapped his arms like a lunatic hawk and crowed, "I'm Austin Gray, and I just love slugs. I do-do. I do-do slugs." Dean-O had finally gone completely out of his freakin' mind, and the parade of kids coming out of the cafeteria slowed down to watch him lose the last of his marbles. "I'm Austin Gray. Watch me do my chicken dance." He flapped some more, then popped his butt out and jiggled it like some rap video hottie. "Gotta shake my tail feathers." Dean jiggled his butt some more. "Doin' the Austin Gray chicken dance. Yes, I am." When Dean finally stopped his tail-wagging, he put his fat, thick hand across his chest and pledged, "I love slugs. I do-do love slugs." Everyone pointed and laughed. But not so much at him. They focused on me. Yet again, I was the real butt of his joke.

I just couldn't stand there and take it anymore. If Maribel could put a stop to her smart-ass hater, then so could I. "STICK IT, DEAN!"

"What did you say to me?" Dean pushed his sleeves up. He had pounded a couple of younger boys and a few others smaller than him, but I'd never heard of Dean Ottmer actually hitting a girl. I backed up a few steps. The student parade entering the building stopped and became an audience. Dean shook his dirty-blond hair out of his face and barked, "What did you say?"

I moved closer to the bench. "I'm, I'm sick of your crap." I was. And it was D-Day for Dean-O even if he hit me. "You're an idiot, Dean, so STICK IT!"

Faster than I could see it coming, Dean Ottmer punched

his arm out and grabbed the skullcap off my head—the purple-and-black check cap, the one Momma had given me for Christmas. "Stick it?" he laughed. "Okay." Then Dean Ottmer did the unthinkable. A personal worst even for him. He stuck my cap down the front of his pants. "You want me to stick it here?" Everyone it seemed, except Maribel, roared. He took it out once and faked handing it back to me. "Here, stork, you can have it back." Then he stuck it down the front of his pants again. He announced, "C'mon, I just do what I'm told." Then he said as loud as he could, "If you want it back, Austin, come and get it. You know where to find it." Dean pushed it farther into his pants, adjusted his crotch, and repeated, "You know where to find it."

Maribel fell onto the bench. I thought she'd fainted. She could stand up to a group of racists but anything remotely sexual caused her brown skin to flare up red like a hot-house tomato. She was a practicing Catholic and still a month away from her *quinceañera*. She fanned herself, then did her best to make me feel better. "That's what too much Red Bull does to a person."

I was a concrete statue in the courtyard as the parade of students filed into the school building. I certainly wasn't Maribel with Mexican revolutionary blood, and I couldn't claim her backup. They were nowhere around. I didn't know what to say or do. If I said anything, Dean would just one-up me. He seemed to have an endless supply of rotten tricks

58

from that gag bag he called a mind. His chicken dance left me exposed and silent in front of the entire lunch crowd.

I might as well have been naked. I had nowhere to go, and every single student pointed, stared, laughed, or all of the above. Several of his "peeps" slapped Dean Ottmer on his back, congratulating him on another successful stunt. Other kids pointed at me, cackling about Dean's outrageous show. Cackling their nervous laughter. Relieved that he hadn't picked on them.

Maribel waited with me while the laughter rolled slowly into the school building. I twisted my scarf, round and round. "Seventy-seven more days." We scooted behind the last of the student parade. "Seventy-seven more days."

"Austin, you don't have to put up with him that much longer." Maribel tried to spin things. "It's not that many more days until school is out."

"It *is* that many more days until the county fair in June," I corrected.

Dean Ottmer won this round, and he could keep my cap. Like I'd ever put it on my head again anyway. But the day was coming when all his stunts and all his insults would spin aimlessly in the air like a fully gassed balloon, unknotted and loosed.

The last two through the double doors into the building, Maribel and I headed down the corridor. A group of blue corduroy jackets and one blond marshmallow girl leaned against lockers at the end of the hall. Thankfully, they had all missed Dean's show. Sundi waved real big at Maribel and me with both hands. Josh slung a backpack over his shoulder, kicked his locker shut with the heel of his cowboy boot, and cut his green eyes at me.

First the county fair, then the sweetheart, I promised myself, then gave a little wave back to the FFA crowd. *The day is coming.*

quince dreams

Maribel stood on the front steps of His Precious Blood Holy Catholic Church in a ballooning, apricot-colored satin ball gown. Honestly, she could've hidden a merry-go-round under that hoop skirt. It was as wide as the old church's Gothic doors. Maribel's black hair was slicked back smooth and wound into a bun at the base of her neck. She had a single lily tucked behind her left ear, and her last doll—her *última muñeca*—cradled in her arms. Today, on her fifteenth birthday, my best friend, Maribel Sanchez, would become a woman.

Momma had closed the store early to help with Maribel's *quinceañera*. She fussed around getting me and the other thirteen *damas* in a line. Maribel gave out strict instructions: tallest to shortest after Marilinda.

Our dresses all matched Maribel's except ours were long and straight instead of full. With my hair up and no shape to the orangey dress, I could've passed for a number 2 pencil. Not the case with Maribel's other friends and her sister, Marilinda. They steamed up the afternoon with their coffee-colored hair and healthy, ba-da-bing curves. I felt out of place. I wasn't Catholic. I wasn't Latina. I was just linear.

A chunky woman in a beaded dress held up a camera. I stood up straight and smiled.

"More like this, Austin." Marilinda turned her back to me, then peeked back over her shoulder with a twinkle. She held her bouquet on her hip, and all the other *damas* followed suit. One long line of red-carpet poses.

I stared at Marilinda's rounded backside. I could've done *more like this* if I had *more like that* to stick out. But I popped my bouquet against my side anyway and flashed my best over-the-shoulder sweetheart smile. Seemed like good practice for next year's no-Jesus parade.

Momma turned to the *escortes*—a huddle of boys some of whom I knew played soccer for Big Wells High. I even sat next to one of them in biology. He kept his eyes closed most of the time. I thought he slept through class, but Maribel said he was trying to translate as the teacher spoke. His long eyelashes fascinated me. They rested on his cheeks like feathery, black fans.

I watched Momma put the boys in order. In the bright sun, their white tuxedos and white fedoras set off the caramel tone in their skin. At that moment, I thought I might actually be able to trill my *r*'s.

"Boys," Momma said. She had on her one dressy outfit: an outdated black suit with a knee-length skirt and old-lady church shoes. The boxy shape of the jacket hid her feminine curves, and she looked like she was wearing someone else's clothes. Out of her jeans and boots, she just didn't look right. "Line up next to your partner," Momma ordered.

They laughed, whispered something in Spanish, then laughed some more. Staring at Momma and me. *Partner*. Not *date* or *girl*, Momma said *partner*. As if it weren't enough for her to hover as the party planner, she took on the job of chaperone as well.

One of the boys lined up next to what I'm guessing was his girlfriend. She giggled, tossing her head back as he eased up behind her, cinched his tattooed hands around her waist, and nuzzled her neck.

"Let's can the PDA." Momma sliced them apart with her arm. "Leave room for Jesus."

Between the laughter and the mumbling, I didn't have to be fluent in Spanish to understand that they thought my momma was a nut. Certifiable. They probably expected it from her by way of town gossip or in-store experience. Then I noticed the boy's hands weren't the only thing tatted up. He had *Jesus* scrawled in ink across the right side of his neck.

I was giving serious thought to ducking under Maribel's hoop skirt when the tallest and skinniest of the escorts did a hip-winding samba in my direction. He wore blue mirrored sunglasses and had a patch of hair shaved into a square on his chin.

Maribel wasn't kidding when she said my escort would be a surprise. She must've found this character in Willy Wonka's chocolate factory. I thought I'd check with her about trading ballroom boy for soccer stud. But when I snapped my fingers to get her attention, she radiated a smile from the church's top step. One of those wide, soul-happy smiles that comes from down deep and lights up the eyes. Her satin dress shimmered in the April afternoon, and she glowed like some sun goddess blessing the day.

I would have to make do.

Mr. Cha-Cha pushed his fedora down low over his forehead and shook to a finale stop in front of me.

"Austin Gray." I stuck my hand out, formally introducing myself.

He stared at it, then pulled me into a chest-hugging tango hold, pressing his brown hand onto my back. I could feel his middle finger inch down my spine. "You dance?" he asked.

"I don't think so!" Momma clopped next to us in her geriatric square-heeled pumps, put her arm around me, and gently pushed him back. "This is a religious occasion," she scolded him. "Mind your manners."

I started to sweat. I didn't think he was cute or anything, but I could still feel his hand between my shoulder blades. I stood stock-still. My escort continued to dance to the Tejano rhythm beating in his own head. Momma smoothed my dress. Then she pulled the off-the-shoulder top more onto my shoulders.

"Austin, I better go in now and take a seat." Momma studied my gyrating escort for a minute, then looked at me. "Are you going to be okay?"

"Of course," I told her.

Momma kissed my cheek and Maribel's, then went inside the church.

"She always like that?" my escort asked.

"Like what?"

"Like hatin' on Mexican boys," he said.

"Gosh, no!" I was horrified. Momma could be a little overprotective. Okay, she was Helicopter Momma—constantly hovering—but she certainly wasn't racist. If she was prejudiced at all, it would be against time. She acted like the more time passed, the further away she was from Daddy. And the closer she was to losing me. It seemed like Momma lived every day trying to control that tension, and I wasn't sure she'd ever come around to letting me go.

A cluster of little girls, each one wrapped in blue and lavender satin with their black hair curled into ribbons on top of their heads, gathered like a garden of Texas bluebonnets in the vestibule. The church doors swung open and the procession for Maribel's *quinceañera* mass began. My escort locked my elbow in his. We followed behind Marilinda, who followed behind the giggling girls.

The soft strumming of a lone guitar resonated inside the quiet church as we filed down the center aisle. The crowd stood. The afternoon sun pierced the stained-glass windows bathing the sanctuary in a pillowy light.

Unlike the First Baptist Church of Big Wells, which could seat half the county and doubled as a disaster shelter, Maribel's church hadn't changed with the times. There was no choir loft or baby grand piano. No microphones. No offering plates. Instead, carved wooden crucifixes hung between each arched window. Lit candles burned hope to a statue of the Virgin Mary. And a prayer-stained altar endured at the feet of her crucified Lord.

Maribel's church was so like her—iconic but real.

I passed Momma, her hands gripping the pew in front of her. Her short, punkish hair looked out of sync with her conservative outfit. So many things about Momma seemed out of sync these last few years.

When we reached the altar, the escorts turned left and we went right—standing in front of the first row of pews. The escorts took off their hats and placed them over their hearts. The guitarist plucked the strings with a flourish, echoing a spirited call to attention throughout the sanctuary. I stared back toward the church's doors, half expecting a mariachi trio to enter. But it was Maribel, anchored on each side by her mother and father, beginning her journey. She seemed to float down the aisle, like a bride on her wedding day.

I squeezed my bouquet in my sweaty palm. The realization that I'd walk without my daddy on my wedding day took hold.

When they reached the pew behind us, her father stepped in. Louis Sanchez loosened the turquoise medallion on his bolero tie. He took out a handerkerchief, dabbing his forehead and his cheeks. Then he settled back into his proud smile.

I guess all fathers do that.

I took my thumb and wiped my wet cheek.

Maribel gave her mother her last doll. Maribel had told me to watch for that. It showed she was putting her childhood behind her. Dolores Sanchez gave her daughter a bouquet of flowers, a kiss on her cheek, and her blessing to head boldly into the world as a young woman.

My momma, Jeannie Gray, stood alone in the back row in her funeral suit and a visible sweat. I wished she could just see Maribel's celebration as a rite of passage for me, too. I was in high school now and going to need some breathing room. I wished my inevitable independence could be easier on my momma.

I wished a lot of things. But for me, a *quinceañera* was just a dream.

Maribel approached the altar and knelt on a pillow. Her apricot gown poofed around her. She crossed her chest and bowed her head. A white-robed priest held out his hands to the audience and began speaking in Spanish. His jackhammer speech, loud and fast, rattled my brain. I picked up a word or two, but I couldn't follow him.

As the priest hammered on, I spotted Raul from the store. He wore a starched white shirt and new blue jeans and held a little girl I had never seen who had fallen asleep on his shoulder. I also caught a glimpse of Daisy Flores, last year's Christmas parade sweetheart for the United Hispanics of Texas. Most of Maribel's attendants and escorts I recognized from school but had never really talked to. These were her people. Los Poblanos.

Even though Maribel and I could finish each other's sentences, I felt like an outsider here. Little Miss Anglo. This wasn't my language. This wasn't my church. And I didn't know all these people. Maribel and I had been friends for what seemed like forever. We shared hair ribbons and bags of Twizzlers and our hearts. But at the end of the day, there was an inexplicable line. When either of us crossed it, we became visitors. We were parallel friends going through life together but in two different worlds.

"Austin." Marilinda tugged on my dress.

The priest had instructed everyone to sit, which they were. I was left standing, like I had an announcement. I played it off, fanning myself with my bouquet as I quietly sunk into the pew. The escorts looked down at their white patent shoes, trying not to laugh out loud at my miscue.

Maribel gathered two fistfuls of her satin skirt and stood. Mamanita, Maribel's wonderfully lumpy grandmother, waddled to the altar, carrying a skinny white box tied with a blue ribbon. She opened the gift, took out a silver bracelet with a dangling cross, and clasped it around Maribel's wrist. Mamanita grabbed Maribel's face, kissed her cheeks over and over, crying happy tears.

I thought about Glammy, my only living grandparent, who was probably sailing on the *Queen Elizabeth II* and stressing over whether or not her shoes matched her handbag.

When Mamanita returned to her seat, the priest placed his hand on Maribel's forehead and prayed. Maribel then carried her bouquet to the altar of the Virgin Mary, placing it as an offering. She crossed her chest and bowed her head. She seemed a million miles away in some distant place and wholly unconcerned that we were all watching her pray.

I counted the wooden squares of the parquet floor. My prayers consisted of nagging God about becoming a hood ornament, thanking Him for necessities like Taco Bell and rain, and outlining problems like Dean Ottmer and death. Maribel's prayer seemed more personal. I felt like we were peeping in on a confessional.

When she returned to the main altar, her mother and a little girl carrying a pillow with a crown stood waiting. Maribel's mother took the lily from behind her daughter's ear and placed the crown upon her head.

"*Triunfante! Triunfante!*" Maribel's mother held her fist in the air as if she'd won some victory, like she'd shot the game-winning basket at the buzzer.

I leaned over to Marilinda. "What's your mom going on about?"

"Triumphant," she whispered. "Maribel has conquered childhood. The crown represents victory and strength for future decisions."

I picked at the lilies in my bouquet. No wonder Maribel had made such a big deal out of turning fifteen. It really was a big deal—more like a graduation than a birthday.

Maribel's father, carrying a pair of three-inch stilettos dyed to match her dress, knelt beside her. He pulled the ballet flats from her feet and Maribel stepped into her first pair of high heels. With her father to escort her, Maribel took her first steps as a woman. He whisked her up the church's aisle and out into the world.

And took my breath away.

With Maribel gone, the crowd crumbled. Men in their bluest jeans and crisp shirts shook hands on their way out the church door. Ladies kissed each others' cheeks. Children ran in circles around the pews. Momma must've been the first out the door. She would be waiting to escort me to the reception.

The *escortes* and *damas* paired up and headed out.

I didn't move.

My escort kept walking. He probably figured my momma would cut him off at the knees.

Marilinda reached back for my hand. "C'mon, Austin," she said. "The reception is the most fun. We've got a DJ and everything. You know Maribel. There will be all kinds of food."

"I'll catch up," I told her as she and the others headed for the reception hall next to the church—the reception where Maribel would waltz with her father.

Alone in the stillness of the church, I snuck up to the altar of the Virgin Mary. I crossed my heart like I'd seen the Catholics do. I wasn't sure what it meant, but it looked prayerful. Then I placed my bouquet next to Maribel's and prayed the problem.

Maribel was dancing a dream I could only dream to dance.

the first compromise

Victor Nesmith campaigned tirelessly for mayor. Posters hung in store windows, yard signs lined neighborhood streets, and two billboards—one on the north side, one on the south side—sandwiched the city of Big Wells. All despite the fact that Nesmith ran unopposed. The only other candidate dropped out of the race early due to an arrest on suspicion of drunk driving. He passed the Breathalyzer test and insisted he was just swerving to miss potholes. He even accused Nesmith and the sheriff of being in cahoots. But the *Big Wells Tribune* put the man's mug shot on the front page of the Sunday paper. His political career was over before it even got going. By the end of May, Nesmith had been reelected and was making good on his promise to have a citywide barbecue and block party in the downtown square.

"He'd trade his eternal soul to the devil if staying mayor was part of the deal," I said, looking at him from the front window of Gray's True Value. Nesmith had the sheriff's deputies setting up barricades to close off the square. He wore a pair of Bermuda shorts and pointed out directions with a longneck bottle.

"Er-eer!" Charles Dickens crowed in agreement. He was as much a part of Gray's True Value now as Momma was. Raul built him a small coop behind the store, but Charles Dickens preferred his perch by the front window. When he got hungry, he'd strut around behind the customers until they fed him. Momma filled an old gumball machine with sunflower seeds and scratch. Customers could turn the knob, and the feed would spill out into their palms. Charles Dickens ate right out of their hands.

"Austin." Momma handed me a broom and a dustpan. "Sweep up the front of the store, then sweep the sidewalk. We did all the business we're probably doing today. With downtown blocked off, I think I'll close the store and do some paperwork." She stood with her hands on her hips, watching Nesmith on the courthouse steps with his beer. "Yeah, I think I'll definitely stay in and get some paperwork done. You go enjoy Victor's barbecue." She closed her eyes, shaking her head. "Sneak me back a plate."

I took my time sweeping the sidewalk, stopping to watch downtown transform into party central. The smoking side of the courthouse, where the employees lit up on their cigarette breaks, was now home to a platform stage for the band and Mayor Nesmith's spotlight. The street across from the stage, along with a few angled parking spaces in front of Wanda's Antique Mall, had been roped off for a street dance. Nesmith had promised a free all-you-can-eat barbecue and live music, but the dance cost ten dollars a person. At each of the square's four intersections, he posted armed sheriff's deputies to collect the dance fee. Nesmith's way of recovering his costs.

"Hey-ey," a voice sang. Sundi Knutt walked up behind me with Josh Whatley and another FFA boy. I dropped my broom. I had gotten used to talking to them at school, but this was unexpected. Seeing them in broad daylight in front of the store kicked the door of possibilities wide open.

"Didn't mean to scare you," Josh said, handing my broom back to me. His T-shirt stretched tight across his chest: SAVE A HORSE, RIDE A COWBOY.

"Lost in thought," I stammered. "Don't, don't you think Nesmith looks like a hairy Jimmy Buffett?" From across the street, we could see the mass of black hair curling out from under the sleeves of his Hawaiian shirt and shorts.

Josh smiled his thin, tight-lipped smile at me. The other boy laughed out loud.

"Jimmy who?" Sundi asked. She had her hands in her back pockets and projected her girls into the conversation. It struck me that she knew full well who Jimmy Buffett was. Asking was simply a way of drawing all eyes back to her.

"You're sure here early for the barbecue," I said, flipping my broom upside down and tapping the handle on the sidewalk. Sundi had the boobs; I had the broom.

"We've been over on the west side of the courthouse all day," the other boy said. He was skinny and bowlegged. He had severely worn down the outside edges of his boots and heels. "We was settin' up the smokers for the barbecue."

Momma opened the door to the store. Charles Dickens came strutting out. He fanned his feathers and clucked. "He needs some fresh air and sunshine," she said. "Let him run around a bit, then put him out back in his coop."

Momma's eyes shifted from Josh to the other boy, then landed on Sundi's blue-polished toenails. Momma glanced up at me like she was trying to solve a complicated math problem. But she seemed to figure it out, because she shook her head and pulled the door to the store shut.

"He's *soooo* cute!" Sundi squealed and reached down for my rooster.

Charles Dickens squawked at the idea of being cute, flew into the street, and charged toward the stage where Nesmith was doing a sound test. I took off after my rooster with Josh Whatley running right beside me. Bowlegged boy shuffled behind us on the sides of his boots. Sundi Knutt, running pigeon-toed, lagged back and harnessed her girls with both arms crossed in front of her chest.

"Testing one, two, three." Nesmith tapped on the microphone with his longneck bottle. "Testing. Testing."

Charles Dickens landed on the stage in a flouncy black cloud of feathers. He stuck his chest out and cocked his beak. The enormous lobes on each side of his head looked like white disc earrings, and his comb was a red patent-leather top hat.

"What the . . . ?" Nesmith downed the rest of his beer and tossed the bottle off the stage. "Austin Gray," Nesmith announced into the microphone. It echoed, "Gray-ay-ay-ay." Charles Dickens belted "HAAAAWK" as loud as I'd ever heard. The speakers carried the crowing all over town. Every time Nesmith spoke, Charles Dickens squawked. All I could hear from Nesmith was the occasional, "DAMN . . . ROOSTER . . . OUT . . . FREAKING . . . POUND." Finally, Nesmith quit trying to talk over Charles Dickens and stepped away from the microphone. Charles Dickens stepped with him. Nesmith moved to the left; Charles Dickens moved to the left. Nesmith moved right; the rooster moved right.

"Looks like you've met your match, Victor," the sheriff said. The deputies and the small crowd that had gathered whistled and cheered. "Your first official dance as the newly reelected mayor is the chicken waltz."

Nesmith stomped his foot and slapped his hands together at Charles Dickens.

Charles Dickens put his head down, like he was looking at something on the ground, but he sidestepped toward Nesmith — edging closer and closer. The rooster popped out a black poof of feathers around his neck.

"He's got his hackles up!" Josh Whatley hopped onto the stage. "He's gonna spur the mayor!"

"CHARLES DICKENS!" I yelled.

The rooster drew his neck feathers back in. Josh reached underneath his breast, gently holding Charles Dickens's legs between his fingers and picking him up. Josh cradled him and rubbed the jiggly wattle under his beak.

"Austin." Nesmith stuck his hairy hand into a cooler by the stage and got another beer. "Your momma and I are gonna have a talk about that rooster." Nesmith was probably looking for an excuse to talk to her anyway. "You better hope it's not one of those illegal fighting cocks."

I bristled. Not so much at his empty threat, but more at the irony of Nesmith using the term *illegal*.

Josh carried Charles Dickens off the stage and through the crowd. I followed him as they cut a path. People were already lining up for the barbecue with their empty paper plates and Styrofoam cups of sweet tea.

"I'm *starving*!" Sundi grabbed the elbow of their bow-legged friend. She stuck out her bottom lip, glossed in bubblegum pink. I bet she had never schlepped her own plate of food through a buffet line.

"I've got to fix my momma a plate, but I better not take him with me."

"You think the Methodist ladies might be offended by a stud rooster going through their barbecue line?" Josh winked at me.

"No." My cheeks burned from his wink. I tried to cover. "Charles Dickens might be offended by the barbecue."

"He's happy with me." Josh rubbed the back of Charles Dickens's long neck. "I'll hold him. You go get your mom's supper."

Bowlegged boy, Sundi, and I got in line with the rest of Big Wells. Red-and-white check cloths draped over long tables. Tin pans heaped with potato salad, baked beans, coleslaw, pickles, and white bread covered the tables. *Maribel would love this*. But she wasn't coming. Nesmith's well-thought-out, campaign-promised, citywide barbecue overlooked the fact that at least a third of the city wouldn't be there. Saturday night was Tejano dance night at the community center. Maribel and Marilinda worked the concession stand and danced. Now that she was fifteen, Maribel's parents allowed her to go. She never missed the Tejano dance; neither did most of her family and friends. Nesmith probably counted on that.

As expected, Sundi didn't carry her own plate. She just sipped on sweet tea and pointed. "Some of that. Yeah, that's good." She'd sip some more on her tea, leaving a pink lip line around the top edge of the cup. "A little of that. No, a little more." Bowlegged boy did an amazing job of juggling his plate and hers. He spread his fingers wide and balanced one plate in each palm. He looked like one of those iron cowboy plant-holding statues with horseshoes for legs.

I loaded Momma's plate up with brisket and coleslaw. "Thanks, Josh." I held her food in one hand and took Charles Dickens from Josh with the other.

"You're coming back, right?"

"Yeah, come back, Austin. We're going to hang out awhile." Sundi perked up and smiled over the pink-kissed rim of her tea. She had been nibbling on a pickle. Food seemed to have a cheerful effect on her. Sundi and Maribel were sure to get along.

I took off for Gray's True Value—weaving in behind Wranglers and boots and out from sundresses and sandals—carrying the plate and the rooster. I put Charles Dickens down in the garden section and ran up the center aisle.

"Here's . . . your . . . barbecue." I tried to catch my breath. "I'm going back outside."

"Whooaa, Nelly!" Momma put her plate on the counter. "What are you going to be doing and with whom are you doing it?"

"The FFA. They asked me to hang out with them." I grabbed her shoulders and hopped up and down. "Pleeeeease." She knew how important hanging with the FFA crowd was to me. We'd be in class together for the next couple of years, and they had been more friendly to me than anyone at school other than Maribel. I wasn't in the automatic friend cliques: band, cheerleading, drill team, sports. Besides, I had my mind set on being the FFA Sweetheart, and their votes would make that happen.

"I've got a couple more hours of paperwork, I guess." She took off her glasses and brushed my bangs with her fingers. "Just don't leave the downtown square."

I rushed out the door—forgetting Charles Dickens on his rake perch at the front of the store, forgetting to put him in his coop.

The sun had gone down and the courthouse square was lit up almost as bright as it was for the Christmas parade. The band kicked into high gear with a rowdy redo of the Dixie Chicks' "There's Your Trouble." From the storefront of

Gray's True Value, I could see Nesmith swaying side to side, off beat from the band. He was tanked, drunk as could be.

I found Josh and Sundi in a group of kids by the barbecue grills and smokers.

"Ya'll know Austin?" Sundi hooked her arm around mine. She smelled powdery like a freshly bathed and lotioned-up baby. I had my doubts as to whether or not she was as innocent as she smelled. But at this moment, I really didn't care. We were connected—last year's FFA Sweetheart and me.

"Let's roll." Josh Whatley came between us. He put his arm around us both. "You can ride with me." Josh stared me right in the eyes. I looked away and swatted an imaginary fly like a complete doofus.

I reined in my spastic fly-swatting and asked, "Where to?" Momma told me not to leave downtown. When she drew a boundary, it may as well have been a razor-wire-topped fence: positively impenetrable. Uncertainty regarding my whereabouts was not a worry she'd tolerate nor was it a worry I'd want to put her through. After Daddy died, I promised myself I'd never leave her wondering where I was or if I was okay.

"Uptown," Josh said. "You know, ride around some." He slid his hand into his jeans front pocket and slipped out his keys. "You comin'?"

"Of course she's coming." Sundi slathered on more lip lube and winked at me.

The FFA kids began walking away from the courthouse

square. A gang of twelve or so, they reminded me of greasers in a book I once read. Not because they had long, greasy hair; the FFA crowd was minus that. They reminded me of greasers because they were outsiders in their own way. Indifferent to chasing fashion fads, comfortable being clean-cut, and too confident to care.

They headed for their trucks and cars parked along the side streets.

"Don't you want to stay and listen to the band?" I asked, hoping they would stick around. But one by one, my sweetheart votes slammed doors, cranked up, and drove away from downtown.

Sundi hooked her arm around mine again. "You need to get to know everyone in FFA." She led me arm in arm behind Josh Whatley down the side street. The band playing on the square sounded farther and farther away. "You never know," Sundi said as we stopped beside Josh's farm truck — a seventies-model, orange-and-white two-tone Chevy — "if your Bantam wins at the fair, you could become next year's sweetheart." Sundi patted my arm, punctuating the possibility.

I climbed into the truck's cab, slowly and somewhat in disbelief at what I was about to do. I wasn't supposed to leave downtown, but I wasn't supposed to lie to my mother either. I was headed down a slippery slope, and I'd brought a sled for the ride. Nesmith had nothing on me. I felt like I was trading my soul to improve my chance at being a hood ornament in the no-Jesus parade. I glanced back at

Nesmith's block party. Couples twirled around the dance floor, ladies from the Methodist church were putting pies where the barbecue had been, and a light was on inside Gray's True Value.

"I'll have to be back in an hour," I told Josh as he scooted behind the wheel. Putting a time limit on my deceit made it seem less shady. "One hour." What could possibly go wrong in an hour?

damage control

Saturday night, and a string of yellow headlights wound up and down Main Street like the chasing flashes on the pinball machine at Pizza Buffet. The circle started at the Dairy Queen, followed Main Street to downtown, rounded the square, then headed back up Main Street to the DQ. Chrome-rimmed cars with subwoofers rattled windows, giant red-and-black trucks jacked up to Jesus rolled on mud tires. Horns honked. Girls squealed. Only two short miles, the circle carried the social life of almost every teenager in Big Wells. And I was riding high center with Josh Whatley, sandwiched between him and Sundi.

It would've been perfect except I didn't have permission to be there.

When the FFA kids got low on gas or tired of driving around, they hung out at a car wash just off Main. Josh Whatley made the circle five or six times before pulling into the car wash. A boy in a black cowboy hat ran up to the truck as soon as Josh put it in park. Josh rolled down the window.

"Hey, man," the boy said, then he spit a brown hocker from under his hat. "Did you hear what just happened to Sammy Ottmer?"

Dean's older brother had been speeding around the circle in his new Ford Mustang. He ran up behind us twice flashing his headlights from dim to bright. Sammy even passed us once on Main Street, nearly hitting an oncoming car head-on.

"Let me guess." Josh turned down Brooks and Dunn and smirked. "The drunk rich boy had a wreck."

The boy in the black cowboy hat rested his arms on the window of Josh's truck. "Big-time," he said.

"Oh my gosh!" Sundi covered her face with both hands. She seemed to have a soft spot for everyone. "Is he hurt?"

I couldn't have cared less about Sammy Ottmer, but I did care about the time. I looked at the dashboard clock. We'd been gone for almost an hour.

"Naw, Ottmer ain't hurt." The boy blew off Sundi's concern. "He's too high to feel hurt from anything. But his Mustang is sure enough screwed up."

"What'd he hit?" Ricky the bowlegged boy asked. He was leaning on his left side, pinned between Sundi's right butt cheek and the passenger-side door. I almost forgot he was in the truck with us.

"You know how downtown is roped off and you have to cut the circle short a block?"

Josh, Sundi, and Ricky all nodded in agreement. I pressed both hands into the dashboard above the clock.

Any drama downtown would give Momma an excuse to hunt for me. I had to get back to the store before she discovered me missing.

"Well," he continued, half laughing, "Ottmer made his own circle. He smashed through a barricade and drove his car straight through the plate-glass window of Gray's True Value."

I jumped across Sundi and Ricky, tried to grab the door handle.

"Oh my gosh!" Sundi put her arm around me, stopped me. Josh patted my leg, then jerked the truck into drive.

"What's the deal?" The boy took off his hat. He looked confused.

Josh nodded toward me. "This is Austin, Austin *Gray*. GRAY'S TRUE VALUE," he yelled as he raced out of the car wash, onto Main Street, and sped downtown.

I dropped my head to my knees, praying and praying like Momma taught me. I prayed the problem, not the outcome. *Lord, Momma is in the store. She doesn't know where I am.* Then I remembered and prayed some more. *I left Charles Dickens on his perch. I should've put him in his coop.* Nothing like praying the problem to bullet-point where a girl went wrong. Maybe that's what praying the problem is all about anyway. Maybe God doesn't change hearts in the solution; he changes them in the problem. *Okay, God. I'm an idiot. I get the consequence for my compromise. But Momma's the only family I've got. . . . She's all I have.*

"I'm sure your mom is okay." Sundi tried to sound convincing. She wouldn't stop rubbing my back and batting her blue-velvet eyelashes at me. Tears swelled in the corners of her eyes. Sundi was a true marshmallow girl, soft all the way through.

Josh skidded the truck to a stop just short of the downtown square. The fire truck and ambulance sealed off Main Street. Josh ran on the sidewalk beside me. I cut between the blocks to the alley behind the store. I could get in from the back door. The dock where Raul loaded wire, and trucks delivered merchandise sat bare and silent. Momma's Jeep and Charles Dickens's empty coop looked abandoned, ghostly under the security light. I stood frozen for a moment in the emptiness. Without Momma, I had nobody.

Josh ran up the steps to the back door. "It's locked!" He twisted and tugged on the knob.

I sprinted out of the alley and headed down the sidewalk toward the front corner of the store.

"Wait just a minute!" The fire chief stepped in front of us. He had on a yellow vinyl coat, and he spread his arms wide. "You kids can't go down there. Get on outta here."

Behind him I could see an ambulance backed up to the curb in front of the store. The band and the dancing couples had stopped. They stood in a mouth-open, head-rubbing, mumbling semicircle behind orange cones and caution tape. Broken glass, twinkling red and yellow in the spinning emergency lights, crunched under police boots. And the turn indicator from the rear of Sammy Ottmer's shiny black, crashed Mustang blinked in what had been the front window of Gray's True Value.

"I'm going to find my momma." I tried to push past the fire chief's outstretched arm.

He grabbed my shoulders and looked at my face. "Austin?"

"Where's my momma? I have to find my momma." I could feel tears welling in my heart, from a place untapped since the Christmas Eve Momma and I waited with cold hot chocolate and fading hope for Daddy to come home. "I have to find—" and the flood of overwhelming uncertainty and crushing loss ran down my cheeks.

"Jeannie's been looking for you, Austin." The fire chief took off his hat. "Your momma's been looking for *you*."

"AUSTIN!" Momma hollered and ran around Sammy Ottmer's rear fender. She wrapped both arms around me. I squeezed her back, making sure she was still in one piece. I just held on.

"Where have you been?" Momma pushed the hair out of my face. "I searched every single clutch of kids around that square."

I looked at her face and a sudden blanket of guilt smothered me. The damage was done. The swollen bags under her eyes were proof of that. My disappearance had brought back all the anxious wondering and helpless hand-wringing that comes when a person you love goes missing. I did that to her. I couldn't hide anything else. "Momma," I began. "I-I wasn't downtown."

She didn't ask me how I could do that to her. How I could bring myself to take her trust and put it on a shelf like a sentimental stuffed animal, treasured but no longer relevant. Momma just smoothed my hair with both hands and kissed my forehead. "We have a mess to clean up," she muttered.

"Ms. Gray," Josh spoke up. "I talked Austin into going uptown, riding around the circle." Sundi and Ricky stood beside him. "It wasn't her idea," he finished.

There was something old-fashioned, Andy Griffith–like about Josh Whatley. Not just his boots and Mayberry manners, but a farm-raised sincerity I had seen only on TV Land in black and white.

"No, Josh." I shook my head. I couldn't let him take the blame. I hadn't been honest about Momma being overprotective. I didn't tell him because I was embarrassed and he was such a good guy he wouldn't have taken me riding around. I didn't ask Momma's permission because she would have said NO. "I wasn't allowed to leave downtown. I should've told you, Josh." I looked at my Momma. "I should've told you, too."

"Jeannie, darlin'!" Frank Ottmer, Dean and Sammy's daddy, barreled toward Momma. He was a thick man with broad shoulders and no neck. His jaws flapped when he walked, and he could've doubled as an English bulldog. Frank Ottmer hugged Momma tight, raising her feet off the ground. "My God, I'm glad you're all right. Austin!" He shot an arm out and yanked me into his grizzly hug. "You girls are both okay. Thank God. Thank God. Thank God." He must've thought saying it three times made it more believable.

"We're fine, Frank." Momma inched out of his clutches. "But I wish you'd get your son's car out of my store."

"Is Sammy okay?" Sundi managed to squeak out.

"Honey, Sammy is going to be just fine, just fine. I'll tell him you asked about him."

That was going to be a task since Frank Ottmer probably had no idea who she was. The reigning FFA Sweetheart didn't run in Sammy's circle of drinking and partying, steroid-juiced friends. None of us did.

"He's cut up a bit," Frank Ottmer continued as if we cared. "I tell ya'll what. I'm calling the Ford company first thing Monday morning, first thing. They may have a recall on their hands if the accelerators are sticking on other Mustangs like the one on Sammy's did."

Momma pulled her hands to her hips in disbelief. Josh and Ricky shook their heads at each other.

"Jeannie." Frank Ottmer glossed over her reaction. "I hate that your store got the worst of it. I sure hate that. But we should all be grateful that Sammy is such an alert driver. He steered that out-of-control car away from the street dance and right onto the curb, right on it."

"Right into the store, Frank." Momma pointed to the corner where Sammy's Mustang sat wedged in the window. "The only thing out of control was your son when he rolled out from behind the air bag with a broken beer bottle in his hand."

"Whoooaa now, whoooaa now, Jeannie." The sheriff spoke to Momma like she was one of the Farhat's spotted donkeys. He had been lurking behind Frank Ottmer the whole time. "Sammy had a root beer, but I didn't find any alcohol in the car."

I rolled my eyes.

Momma just stared at him, burned a hole right through him.

"Give me a break," Josh said. He leaned against the side of the building with one foot on the sidewalk, the other foot flat against the wall.

"Jeannie." Frank Ottmer tried putting his arm around Momma again. She stepped out of his reach. "You're all right. Sammy's all right. Nobody's hurt." He had check-book confidence and was in full damage-control mode. "I've already called the glass company. They're gonna fix that front window tomorrow, even though it's a Sunday, to your specifications and satisfaction." He pulled his fat wallet from his back pocket. "There's no need to call the insurance company, no need." Frank Ottmer pinched a credit card between two fingers and flicked it toward Momma. She didn't budge. "Even though the damage is nobody's fault"—he forced his point—"I mean it's *nobody's* fault, I want you to charge to this card any and all of the replacement costs of that yard stuff destroyed in the crash."

"What yard stuff?" I demanded.

Frank Ottmer seemed frustrated. "All those rakes and things on that display behind the window."

My stomach flipped. *Things?* What *things?* I was plummeting, like a sick free fall on a theme park roller coaster. "Where's Charles Dickens?"

"Didn't you put him in his coop?" Momma asked. "I was in the back of the store doing paperwork when the car hit, Austin."

I darted past two sheriff's deputies and around the back end of the car jutting from the window. The front door of Gray's True Value was open and the lights were on. Mayor Nesmith, a woman in a county-issued uniform, and several men stood around the center aisle. They all looked up when I walked in.

Shards of broken wedding china and fancy crystal littered the bridal registry side of the front of the store. The garden tool display on the other side had fallen onto the hood of the car. Charles Dickens's rake perch lay on the wood floor underneath the chrome-rimmed front tire of Sammy Ottmer's Mustang.

I pulled a black feather out of the car's grille. Momma, Josh, Frank Ottmer, and the sheriff piled into the store.

"Have you seen my rooster?" I moved toward Mayor Nesmith.

"Your rooster is not harmed," the uniformed lady said. She wore a white patch sewn over the shirt pocket: ANIMAL CONTROL. "He's distressed and out of control. The mayor says he tried to attack him. We're going to quarantine him for a few weeks." She and the mayor stood side by side. Behind them, on the floor, Charles Dickens huddled in a cat caddy. He had been confiscated and incarcerated.

I rubbed the sweat from my palms onto my jeans. "What you're going to do is give me my chicken," I demanded, hitting bottom on my imaginary coaster and shooting back up.

"You better check yourself, young lady." Nesmith dizzily waved a hairy finger at me. He was still drunk. "As mayor I have an *obligination* to the citizens. This *wooster* is not only an *aggreshive* threat to the *pubic*, but also he is a farm *aminal* inside the *cimy litits*. We have no choice but to pound him, in the pound." Nesmith punched his right fist into his left palm.

I felt Momma's hand grip my shoulder, pulling me back.

"Victor." Momma eased between the mayor and Miss Animal Control. Momma reached between them and picked up the pet caddy. "We'll get this carrier back to you next week."

"So, s-s-sorry, Jeannie," Nesmith stammered. "The *wooster* is *histree*."

Momma strolled back to the broken storefront, stopping in front of Frank Ottmer and the sheriff and carrying the pet caddy in one hand. I bent down beside the cage. Charles Dickens gripped a blue claw around the metal grate. I rubbed his leg with one finger.

Momma pulled her shoulders back. She had *dare-me* posture and a sobering, priceless confidence. "Nothing happens to this rooster." She stared at the sheriff, then locked eyes with Frank Ottmer. "Are we all clear?"

Frank Ottmer tapped the sheriff on the back. "Go help the mayor understand that the rooster is the Grays' pet, their family pet. There's no animal to control."

The sheriff winked at Frank Ottmer, dismissed Miss Animal Control, and guided Nesmith out of Gray's True Value.

A tow truck came and pulled Sammy Ottmer's Mustang out of the window. Even more glass crashed and crunched. Frank Ottmer left with the car and his credit card.

We released Charles Dickens into his coop behind the store. Raul had hung a wooden rod from the tin roof. Charles Dickens sailed right to it. He didn't touch the scratch or the fresh water that Sundi took such care in placing in his coop. The trauma had been too much for him; he was stressed and missing a few feathers. Four weeks away from the county fair, Charles Dickens was in no shape to show.

No one said much. Josh, Sundi, and Ricky stayed late and helped Momma and me clean up. In addition to sending Frank Ottmer packing with his Band-Aid bucks, Momma had turned down his offer to pay for a crew of helpers. The FFA crew, however, didn't bother offering; they just went to work. Josh and Ricky moved the bigger stuff: dented display shelves, stacks of galvanized buckets, wheelbarrows. Momma took a broom handle and shattered the leftover jagged glass protruding from around the window frame. Then she flipped the broom over and went back to sweeping. Sundi put on a pair of leather work gloves and picked up large, broken shards of glass too big to sweep. She dropped them one by one into a heavy-duty trash bag. I sorted merchandise, the damaged from the undamaged.

Frank Ottmer was certainly a man of action. By Sunday evening, the plate-glass window had been replaced. The new glass, clean and clear, fit snug in the old wood frame. Now only the front door and other window rattled in the wind. What had been broken and shattered—the visible stuff—was now cleaned up, fixed up, good as new. But no matter the cleanup and repair, the damage had been done. Things never go back exactly as they were before.

10
movin' on

The distance between me and Momma seemed as dark and long as the hallway stretching from my bedroom door to the den where she sat lacing up her running shoes. I watched her in the early morning moonglow, and I wanted to tell her how sorry I was for leaving downtown, for putting her through such worry.

"Momma," I half whispered.

"I'm going jogging, Austin." She tugged her laces taut and twisted them into double knots.

"I'm going, too." I started down the hall. I'd been in my shorts and tennis shoes since way after midnight when I finally realized I couldn't rest until Momma and I had gotten squared up.

Momma squinted her eyes at me. She looked me up and down.

"Look, Austin." She never minced words. "I know you're sorry for not minding and making me look all over for you in the middle of that disaster of a night. But that's over with and today is a new day." She pointed out the window. The blue morning was giving up to daybreak.

I spent half the night rehearsing exactly what I wanted to say. And since I had nothing left to lose, I got the notion that maybe I could get her to talk about Daddy, too. We seemed just fine discussing everything else. Now seemed like the right time to put it all out on the table. I swallowed hard. "I just wanted us to talk about it, to straighten—"

Momma cut me off before I could finish.

"There's no *it* and nothing to straighten." Momma patted my back and walked to the door. "I'm going about two miles today. You can come with me if you want."

I followed her. She might shut me up for the moment, but I wasn't going away. Momma was all I had, and I wasn't about to let her shut me out.

Except for a few singing birds and the click-click-woosh of sprinklers, Camellia Heights was dead quiet this early in the morning. Momma took off into the neighborhood with long strides like she was running from something and if she slowed down she just might have to face it.

I stayed back about twenty yards. Momma and I never ran side by side; I always trailed, even when she was helping me train for cross-country. She said it was safer that way. If we ran next to each other, one of us would be in the middle of the road. Too risky. If she said it once, she said it a hundred times: Side by side is too risky.

We'd jogged about a quarter of a mile toward the turn-around at the end of Camellia Heights. The top of the sun stuck up over the old magnolia trees that ran alongside the Ottmers' place. The thick branches reached up like a big hand grabbing at the day. Momma's strides shortened. She stopped just at the edge of Dean Ottmer's driveway. Momma never broke stride for anything. She'd hop on a curb or jog in place on a corner, but she never just stopped. And we were just getting started. I sprinted toward her.

As I got close to the Ottmers' place, I spotted the back end of a new Ford truck angled on the grass just off the driveway. The truck was so new it had a paper license plate stuck on the window and no permanent tags. It had a boat hitched to it, and I could tell the boat had clipped one of the brick columns anchoring the entrance to the Ottmers' drive. A big chunk of brick was missing and the light on top of the column was busted. I ran up the drive.

Momma held her hand up for me to stop. "Stay back, Austin."

The driver's-side door of the truck was open. I saw Sammy Ottmer slumped over the wheel with nothing on but a pair of flip-flops.

I grabbed ahold of the tailgate and tried to look away. "Sammy?"

No response.

"Sammy," Momma repeated.

I stole a glance out of the corner of my eye. Dozens of beer cans littered the truck bed. A cooler lay on its side with red Jell-O packets and a broken bottle of vodka crunched in front of it. The sticky mess smelled like the bathroom at the Big Wells Little League Park.

Momma stood just out of the door frame and yelled, "Sammy!"

A groan came from the truck. Through the back window, I watched Sammy roll his head around.

"Oh, God!" Sammy moaned.

Momma jumped back.

Sammy Ottmer fell face-first out of the truck, heaving and puking. On all fours. Butt naked.

I had to grab the tailgate to keep from fainting.

"Austin, go on home. You don't need to witness this," Momma said. "I think he's going to be okay. I'm going to get his folks."

Sammy might be okay, but I was going to need my brain bleached. His tan-outlined lily-white backside was stamped into my head. Watching naked Sammy squirm on the ground next to his own vomit shored up my resolve to just say NO to drugs and alcohol.

I jogged the short distance back home and waited for Momma. I made Momma her pot of coffee and waited. I tried not to think about Sammy. Catching him naked was a shocker, but finding him drunk wasn't. Sammy's drunk summers were as expected as the Texas heat.

Trying to get my mind off of naked Sammy, I practiced apologizing to Momma and even asking her about Daddy. When she walked through the door, I was ready.

"Is Sammy still alive?" I asked.

"For now," she answered. "But if his parents don't wrangle him in and take his vehicles and boat away, he's going to wind up killing himself in—" Momma stopped in mid-sentence.

I poured her a cup of coffee.

"Momma," I started. "I think Sammy does things and he doesn't give a rip what his parents think."

Momma slowly stirred her coffee. In the morning light, the marionette lines drawing the corners of her mouth downward showed.

"Well." I took a deep breath. "Not every kid is like that. And I'm going to tell you that I'm really sorry for all the trouble I caused whether you want to hear it or not."

"You've done that now, and I've told you everything is okay." Momma untied her shoes, picked up her coffee, and headed for the shower. "Forgive yourself, Austin. And move on. You've got the fair in four weeks and a lot of preparing to do for that." Just like that, she disappeared into her bedroom.

Discussion over.

Our old house hummed when the water from the shower came on. Momma talked a lot about moving on. But I looked around the kitchen. Neither one of us ever sat in Daddy's chair at the table. His tools were still in the garage. Momma's wardrobe was black except for blue jeans. She was a walking bruise. She moved on about all sorts of daily trials, but Daddy's death was different. She loaded that up and carried it with her.

showstopper

Prosper County Fair officials would judge all the live-stock according to its Standard of Perfection. For Bantams, that included being clean and calm. Charles Dickens was neither. Distressed from the terror of Sammy Ottmer's drunken drive-through, my rooster thrashed madly and daily in a dirt hole in the backyard. When the dust settled, Charles Dickens looked like a black ball of frayed yarn batted around by WhizBang the cat.

"Maybe I should just enter him in the crowing contest." I watched Charles Dickens flail out of control in the dirt. Without him, I had no FFA project and no shot at making it into the no-Jesus parade.

But Maribel wouldn't let me give up.

"Austin, he's the prettiest bird in the county," she said.

I looked at Charles Dickens. He had a clump of dirt on the end of his beak, and he flapped about crazily shaking his head side to side, trying to toss the dirt off. He finally just stuck his head back in the hole and spun around.

I buried my head in my hands. Defeat hung in the air like the stench wafting off a dairy barn's manure mounds.

"Something's not measuring up." Maribel sat with her feet up on a beach towel in Momma's glider. The June sun turned the metal glider into a hot skillet. She flipped through one of my how-to chicken-raising books. "There has to be an explanation for his half-baked behavior."

"Sammy Ottmer *drove* him crazy. That's what happened." I thought about getting in the hole with Charles Dickens. Dean Ottmer had pushed me to a sanity-snapping point more than once. Now my hope of riding in the no-Jesus parade—of being sweetheart and giving Dean-O the up-yours, princess wave-off—kicked around in a cloud of dust.

"Parasites!" Maribel announced.

"Yes, they are." I pointed over the fence and up the street toward the Ottmers.

"Not them. Charles Dickens. He's dusting." Maribel started reading out loud. "Chickens dust themselves by lying on their sides and flapping around in the dirt. That's how they get rid of parasites and stay clean."

"He doesn't have bugs!" I cringed at the very notion that Momma and I would have a dirty chicken. "I check for mites and lice every two weeks, and the vet comes in the store at least once a month. Momma has him check out Charles Dickens every time." I had done my job—spending the last five months keeping him clean and making sure he would handle easily. I had too much riding on him. "I

100

would've known if he had parasites, Maribel. Besides, don't you think he would've been flapping around like that since last Christmas if that's what was wrong with him?"

"Maybe he has been." Maribel pulled a pack of sunflower seeds from her pocket. "We've only been out of school on summer break one week. And I think they dust whether or not they actually have parasites. He probably did it all spring. We just weren't around to see it." She poured the sunflower seeds into her hand. "There are a couple of holes in his run behind the store."

Charles Dickens flew onto the glider beside Maribel. She stuck her hand out, letting him peck at the seeds. "Keep training him, Austin. It's like kneading bread dough: If you work it just right, it'll rise."

Even though he'd been acting like a loony bird, Charles Dickens still had the right stuff to be a champion. He definitely did not have parasites, and he had no defects. His full frock of feathers looked a rich black despite the dirt. And most days, he was more lapdog than boss cock—very easy to handle. Maribel was right. Charles Dickens was a winner. And if his dirt-hole flailing was just normal chicken behavior, he was still on track to make Prosper County Fair history, and I was still on track for sweetheart. All my rooster really needed was a little last-minute show training. With Maribel's help, I began to put Charles Dickens through show bird boot camp.

I brought out his show coop, a wire cage the size of a laundry basket.

"The judges have to take him in and out," I explained. "He needs to be calm and easy to handle." I had spent most of the spring semester studying chicken fancy. I got a B in English, but I could quote word for word the American Bantam Association's Standard of Perfection.

I picked up Charles Dickens and put him in the cage. "When you take him out, put one hand under his breast and the other over his wings. Pull him out headfirst." I scooted back, giving Maribel a try. "If you pull him out backwards, he might try to get loose. He's supposed to look at your face."

"He doesn't seem to mind this," she said. Charles Dickens came out with no problem. He even let her push his beak up to check his wattle and pull his feathers back to check his wings. She held him in one hand, looking him over just like the judges would do. Spending most days at Gray's True Value and being handled by the customers kept Charles Dickens gentle. Maribel placed him back in his coop, headfirst.

"He's going to need a bath, too," I said. Charles Dickens had a dusty brown powdering of dirt from the tip of his comb to the bottom of his blue shanks.

Maribel and I carried him into the laundry room and filled the sink with warm water. I added a couple of squirts of Momma's Lady Primrose bubble bath. Maribel dipped her finger in the sudsy water.

"Just right," she said. "You want simmered chicken, not boiled."

I placed both hands over Charles Dickens's wings and lowered him up to his neck into the suds. He didn't flinch. I pushed and pulled him like a swinging pendulum through the bath, letting the soapy water run through his feathers. Maribel gently scrubbed his shanks and claws with Momma's manicure brush.

We rinsed him three times, the last using the sink sprayer, then double-wrapped him in a beach towel. Charles Dickens peeked his red-crowned, black head out from the towel. Maribel stroked his comb, cuddled him, and took him outside into the sunshine.

I sat down next to her on the glider.

"This is half alcohol, half water." I held up a coffee cup and a box of Q-tips. "I need to clean his comb and wattle."

I passed the Q-tip over and under, in and around his rose comb and jiggly wattle until every speck of dirt was gone. We put him back in his show cage to let him dry outside. Maribel and I put on our swimsuits and sunned ourselves on the patio with him. WhizBang crouched on the corner fence post. We weren't about to leave Charles Dickens alone.

"I'm caramelizing." Maribel scooted her chaise into the shade. She pulled Charles Dickens from his cage, headfirst like we'd trained him. He sat motionless in her lap, his feathers soaking up the sunlight and shining like black glass. Maribel squirted a tiny dot of coconut suntan lotion in her hand. She massaged it into his comb and wattle, and over his shanks.

"Er-eeeer," Charles Dickens crowed and sailed onto the back of the glider. His drying feathers fluffed in the wind. He popped his raven chest out, proudly flashed his white lobes, and fanned his wings, showing off the silky clean plumage. He looked down his beak at WhizBang sitting powerless on the fence post.

"What a snob!" I laughed at Charles Dickens's haughty perch.

"He's a real showstopper," Maribel said.

Indeed he was a real showstopper — Bantam Perfection.

> Weight: 26 ounces.
> Comb: bright red, firm, and even on head.
> Lobes: large and white.
> Wattles: no wrinkles and firm.
> Head: carried proudly.
> Back: from neck to tail, one long curve.

Charles Dickens was way better-looking than that porker Sundi won with last year. No doubt, Charles Dickens had blue ribbon written all over him.

And the judging was about to begin.

12
fair game

Charles Dickens and I strutted into the Poultry Tent just before time to coop in. He was in full bloom with a bounty of feathers and a showtime attitude. I stepped onto the hay-covered ground in my new cowboy boots, polished black just like my rooster.

"You can't go traipsing through hay-filled tents and barns in sandals," Momma had said when she gave them to me. The boots were her way of making sure I understood she wasn't holding anything against me.

"Show birds go to Section D." A worker pointed to the gigantic capital letters hanging from the tent's roof.

"Thanks."

The Poultry Tent was one big coop filled with lots of fat white hens and poults and Bantams and turkeys. I recognized some of the FFA students from school, one girl struggling to hang on to a nervous turkey. Most of the teenagers and students I didn't know. They came from surrounding counties and towns in hopes of their fowl winning. Everyone, it seemed, wore boots and jeans with silver belt buckles the size of horses' hooves. I went the cute route: my new boots and a denim mini. And my hair pulled into a ponytail with a black silk ribbon.

I sauntered up to Section D.

"Name and class?" A woman held a clipboard full of labels and a Sharpie.

"Austin Gray," I said. "Rosecomb Bantam, Clean-Legged."

"Clip this to the cage, and place the rooster next in line on Table 3." She handed me the label.

I sized up the competition. Out of the seven Rosecombs on the table, six were white. The other rooster had black specks all over and looked thin, like he could benefit from a few slugs. I could hardly contain myself. No rooster on that table could come close to beating Charles Dickens.

"Hey, baby," a low voice rumbled. "How 'bout scootin' over, baby, and givin' big daddy some room."

Standing next to me in white patent-leather shoes was a chubby boy stuffed like a sausage into a white jumpsuit with flared bell-bottoms. The gold-trimmed collar stood up around his neck, then dropped in a chest-open V down to his first fat roll. His black hair was slicked back, and he adjusted his oversized sunglasses with ring-covered fingers. He was the worst Elvis impersonator I had ever seen, but he was carrying the most colorful Bantam rooster I had ever laid eyes on.

He sat his caged rooster on the table next to Charles Dickens. It had a black breast and long, sickle-like black feathers shooting out from its tail. In that way, it resembled Charles Dickens. But draped across its neck and saddle was a blanket of red-orange feathers that made that rooster outstanding. He looked like my rooster but with a flashy flaming shawl. Even Charles Dickens stared.

"This is *The King*." The boy nodded toward his cage and stuck out a sweaty hand. "I'm Elvis, baby."

"The cage tag says Lewis Fortenberry." Then I recognized him from school. He was in the band, and I remembered how Dean Ottmer made fun of him in the No-Jesus Christmas Parade. I gave him my best limp handshake. "That makes you an Elvis *impersonator*."

"Elvis Performance Artist," he corrected. Then he wound his right arm around in the air and popped his hips. He stopped his arm and pointed at Charles Dickens. "That your rooster?"

"Sure is." I didn't really want to talk to him at all. I knew of his family. They grew blue-ribbon fruit and were Prosper County farming royalty. I wished he'd just take his flame-necked fowl and go home.

"Your rooster's a shoo-in for second place." Elvis smiled at Charles Dickens.

I regretted ever feeling sorry for Lewis Fortenberry. Any fat boy confident enough to show up at the county fair dressed as Elvis would have been unfazed by Dean Ottmer's belittling imitation.

"My rooster hasn't lost yet, Lewis."

I folded my arms and stared at his rooster. The King

might be a little fat, which is a point deduction. His comb was good, but his beak could've been trimmed some. Another point deduction. Lewis practiced taking him in and out of his cage. He was as easy to handle as Charles Dickens. First place was going to come down to the judge's personal preference.

The shuffle of boots scooted behind me in the hay. They whispered to a stop. Someone breathed over my shoulder.

"Gonna come down to the airs."

I whipped around. Lafitte Boudreaux stood there—hands in his pockets, hat pulled low over his eyes. "Miss Aus'in, ya sho' is jumpy. Ah do believe ya's the jumpiest gal Ah ever did know."

I put my hand over my heart. "You just snuck up behind me's all." He gave me a fright, but I was glad to see him. "What do you think?" I picked up Charles Dickens, drawing him headfirst from his cage.

Mr. Boudreaux held him in one hand. "Ya done a good job." He smiled, showing two gold teeth. "Ya sho' done a good job. He ain't no stressed bird and he got full bloom on." Mr. Boudreaux handed Charles Dickens back to me. "That'un gonna be in the runnin', too." He pointed at The King.

"You think the one with more color will win?" I asked, hoping for a "no way."

" 'Pends on the airs. They both some pretty, so it gonna come down to showin' out. They gots to be alert, lookin' around."

The King pranced around in his cage. His robust chest

was thrust out and his eyes darted around the tent. Charles Dickens's eyes were heavy, like he needed a nap. Mr. Boudreaux dug around in his pocket and pulled out a jar of Vicks VapoRub.

"Dab yo' finger in dis here." He twisted off the lid. The mentholatum smell burned my nostrils and made my eyes water. "Rub a little, right here on his wattle." Mr. Boudreaux rubbed two fingers over the bump in the middle of his neck. "That'll give him the look-arounds."

"Attention, Bantam Table 3." An announcement blared over the loudspeakers. "Judging in fifteen minutes."

I quickly dipped a finger in the menthol rub and massaged a dab into Charles Dickens's wattle. He woke up. His nostrils flared and the light in his eyes flashed.

"Game on," I declared now that my rooster had perked up.

I closed the cage door and turned around. Lafitte Boudreaux was gone. In his place, wearing baggy shorts and untied tennis shoes, Dean Ottmer stood with his usual crowd of hangers-on.

"Looks like we've found the stork competition," Dean said, staring at my legs.

As expected, the boys supported him with laughter.

Goose bumps ran up my thighs. I wanted to hide.

"Dean-O!" Lewis Fortenberry saved me. He spun around in his jumpsuit with his sunglasses on. "Cruising for chicks, baby?"

"Fortenberry, you fat freak!" Dean had warmed up on me. Now he reared up for an all-out assault on Lewis. "Being a band weenie not gay enough for you?" Dean's jokers snorted with laughter. "How 'bout you sing 'Love Me Tender' to that rooster?"

Lewis was twice Dean's size, and I wished he'd go WWE on him—come off the top rope and flatten Dean to the mat. But he didn't. Lewis didn't even seem embarrassed. He just channeled Elvis.

"Pull my finger, Dean-O, baby." Lewis shook one leg and held his index finger at Dean.

I had seen boys do the "Pull My Finger" fart joke before. But this was the first time I had seen anyone pull a joke on Dean. As far as I was concerned, Dean Ottmer was fair game. His face went red when even his own goons chuckled.

"Hah!" I blurted. It just popped out like a jack-in-the-box when Jack had been shoved down and the lid slammed. Lewis's joke let it loose.

Dean turned his hate back on me. "You think that's funny? Well, I think it's funny that the Fortenberry Fruit Fairy here has more cleavage than you do." Dean patted the bare chest between the V of Lewis's jumpsuit. Then he and his howling band of wolves went trolling out of the Poultry Tent.

The goose bumps swarmed all over. What little flesh I had that passed for boobs shriveled to nothing inside my A-cup Wonderbra.

"Don't let him get to ya', baby." Elvis put his arm around me.

My eyes started to water. I didn't want him to feel sorry for me. To me, sympathy was like alcohol on a scraped knee. It didn't really heal anything; it just made the injury sting.

"Dean makes fun of everyone." Lewis found his own voice. "He builds himself up by putting others down. That's all he's got. He's a big nothing behind that mouth."

I tried drying my eyes with my hands, but I just spread the wet. Lewis held up a sleeve. "Use this," he said. So I dried my eyes on Elvis's white jumpsuit.

"You gotta do your own thing, Austin." Lewis then belted out some Elvis song about dreaming the impossible dream. Belted it at the top of his lungs. He spread his arms wide on the dream part, and the whole tent stared.

Lewis made me laugh out loud and he stuck it to Dean Ottmer. I decided right then that Lewis and I would be all right even if his gaudy rooster beat me.

"Attention, Bantam Table 3," the announcer blared again. "Judging in five minutes."

I wiped my hands on my skirt and pulled Charles Dickens from his cage. He was wide-eyed and alert, thanks to Lafitte Boudreaux's last-minute VapoRub.

"Okay, Charles Dickens." I placed him on the table and checked him over one last time. No dirt in his claws. Eyes bright and clear. Neck up. Chest out. He fanned his feathers and ruffled them. "And freshly fluffed. Good boy." I massaged his wattle and comb, kissed his beak, and put

Charles Dickens back in his show cage. He strutted around, working it like a catwalk diva.

"It's on, Lewis!" I grinned at him. He was putting The King back in his cage.

"Yes it is, little momma." Lewis spoke into his pretend microphone.

A woman in a blue blazer stepped in front of the tables. She raised her eyebrows when she saw Lewis's rooster. Not a good sign for me and Charles Dickens.

"I'd like for the owners to step away from their Bantams and gather to my left."

Lewis and I joined the others. Momma, Josh Whatley, and Sundi entered the tent and made their way toward us. Sundi held up a first-place ribbon in one hand and a Grand Champion ribbon in the other. Her smile brightened the whole tent. She had entered a lamb this year instead of a sow. I was glad it won. She had raised it like a baby, hand-feeding it from a bottle.

"I'm going to score each rooster individually according to the American Bantam Standard," the judge explained to us. "I will compare it first to the ideal or standard for Rose-comb, Clean-Legged Bantams. Then I will rank the roosters. In case of a tie, weight will fall with showmanship. I will discuss the placings when the judging is over. Please wait quietly with your family and friends."

"I'm glad you made it." I hugged Momma.

"Raul will keep the store running." She kissed my forehead. "I wouldn't have missed this for anything."

"Look at you, Miss Grand Champion!" I took Sundi's ribbons and ran my fingers over them. I wasn't surprised that Sundi's lamb won. It was snow white except for its black face and black feet. The lamb looked chocolate-dipped.

"Snow Angel showed beautifully. All the judges loved her. We'll have our picture taken together after you win." Sundi reassured me by putting her arm around my waist.

"Hey, baby." Elvis made a move on Sundi. "Share some love with the teddy bear." He took her other arm and put it around his gold-sequined belt.

"What the heck?" Josh laughed. Momma did, too.

"Ya'll know Lewis Fortenberry?" I asked.

Sundi rolled her big blue eyes. "You're an Elvis impersonator?"

"Performance artist, baby. Elvis Performance Artist." He raised a ring-covered hand in the air and twisted his hips. "The grandstand, today at five. A show you don't want to miss."

"Lewis also has the Bantam next to Charles Dickens. The pretty one." I cringed when they all chimed, "Wow."

"Sorry, Lewis." Josh reached out and held my hand. "I don't think it can beat Austin's rooster. Charles Dickens is right perfect."

For a moment, I forgot I was in the Poultry Tent. Josh Whatley was holding my hand. I had been certain we were friends like he and Sundi. But this didn't feel like friend hand-holding; the goose bumps came back on my legs. Momma was watching. I took my hand back.

"Has anyone seen Maribel?" I pretended to fix the latch on Charles Dickens's cage.

"She's still waiting on the ice-cream results," Momma said. "I checked on her before I came in here." Momma kept talking even though chitchat wasn't her thing. She knew I was uncomfortable, so she tried. "If you ask me, her Mango Kick was the best ice cream I tasted—kind of sweet-hot with the fruit and the red pepper."

"I hope Maribel wins," Sundi said. She had a starry-eyed sweetness about her that made me jealous. I couldn't imagine Sundi without her bright outlook. Maybe that's what happens when a girl becomes sweetheart. She's responsible for the optimism of those around her. Note to self.

"If I could get the owners to stand behind their roosters, please." The judge held a stack of ribbons.

Lewis and I moved toward the table. Momma stopped me.

"Win or lose." She smiled into my eyes. "Feel good about what you've accomplished. That's where real confidence is."

I stood behind Charles Dickens's cage. Lewis twisted his way behind The King. Maybe he was always that confident, but he acted like first place had Lewis Fortenberry written all over it.

The judge passed up and down in front of the cages twice. On her second pass, she placed a third-place ribbon on the cage of a Milk White Rosecomb with downy feathers.

Then she stopped between Lewis and me.

I twirled the curl on the end of my ponytail.

The judge held a red second-place ribbon in her right hand and a bright blue, ruffled first-place in her left. Charles Dickens and I were in front of her right hand.

"Ladies and Gentlemen." She raised both ribbons in the air.

Momma stood rigid, with her hands pressed against her thighs like a Marine—her signal for me to stand up straight and quit twirling my hair.

"First place goes to . . . Austin Gray!" She crossed her hands in the air and placed the blue ribbon onto Charles Dickens's cage.

I rocked back on the heels of my boots and raised my hands into the air. "YES!"

Lewis gave me a giant sweaty armpit hug and genuine congratulations. Momma pulled Charles Dickens from his cage and put him in my arms.

"Way to go, boy!" I held him close and rubbed his wattle. We were winners, Charles Dickens and I, champions. I was the phoenix of the Poultry Tent, on fire and rising strong. FFA Sweetheart just might be mine for the plucking.

"I'm proud of you, Austin." Momma squeezed me and Charles Dickens. "You went for it. You saw it through. You made it happen."

Her voice was low, mechanical. Not quite the reaction I expected. And the corners of her mouth turned down. Momma said all the right things, but her face told a different story.

"Momma, what's—" I started.

Then Maribel stomped up, toting a cooler with her ice cream in it. She had on her Mexican floral fiesta dress. The one made out of white cotton with colorful flowers embroidered all over. She sat the cooler on the ground and took Charles Dickens. "I knew he'd win." She kissed his comb.

"How'd you come out?" I took my eyes off Momma for a minute and searched all over the turquoise, purple, and orange flowers of Maribel's dress for a ribbon.

"Didn't even place," Maribel said. "The top three were Lemon Burst, Chocolate Kiss, and Old-Fashioned Vanilla. Blah. Blah. Blah." She pooh-poohed the results. "Mango Kick was too Mexican, way too ethnic. One of the church-lady judges called it Hellfire ice cream."

"Unbelievable!" Momma had her hands on her hips. "This is turning into the county *un*fair."

"No worries." Maribel massaged Charles Dickens's wattle. "I don't need them to prove my ice cream is good. I know it's good. And they'll be gossiping about it all over town. People will call me, wanting to buy it like they do Mamanita's *pico de gallo*. I probably *should* call it Hellfire ice cream. I'm kind of liking that, actually." Maribel stopped talking and took a long look at Lewis. "What's up, Elvis?"

I glanced around. Sundi and Josh had disappeared. They were nowhere in sight. I had won and they didn't even stick around. No cowboy hand-holding. No marshmallow-girl hugs.

"Where'd Sundi and Josh go?"

Momma had two lines between her eyebrows, her "drainpipes." I could always tell how worried she was by their depth.

"You know you won a premium, a fifty-dollar cash prize for Charles Dickens?" Momma hesitated. I could tell she was holding something back.

Lewis picked at the gate on The King's cage. Elvis had suddenly developed a case of the blues. Maribel handed Charles Dickens back to me.

"Show birds are different from some of the other animals." Momma rested her hand on my shoulder.

Lewis looked up at the top of the tent and put his gold-rimmed sunglasses back on.

"Right," I said. I knew market animals, those used for meat and breeding, earned their owners money, sometimes several thousand dollars. FFA students were known for paying for college with their earnings. Recognizing the animals as pets, most buyers returned them to the kids. The money was just a way of encouraging students in the business of agriculture.

"Someone bought Sundi's lamb," Mom continued. "They paid three thousand dollars for it."

"That's great, isn't it?"

"Return it or ship it." Lewis flicked the lock on The King's cage.

"They returned Snow Angel to her, didn't they?" I rubbed Charles Dickens's belly. His heart beat steady in my hand.

"The FFA teacher came and got her during your award. He gave her the check, but the buyer for Sundi's lamb chose to ship," Momma said, letting out a deep breath. Lewis poked around in the hay with the point of his patent leather shoe. "They put her lamb on the meat truck. It's going to the butcher."

anger management

Neon carnival lights blinked on and off in the fair's midway. Heavy metal guitars screeched from the fun house. Some sunburned kid fingering a funnel cake stepped in front of me. I leveled him.

"I'm sorry!" Yelling would have to do. I kept running, kept looking for Sundi. With each step, my boots hit the ground hard, kicking up dust.

I found Sundi in the roped-off field between the Tilt-A-Whirl ride and the demolition derby arena: the skillet-throwing contest. The sun was an orange ball dropping in the June sky and Sundi, casting a long shadow, stood with her legs spread, holding a ten-inch cast iron skillet above her head. She was getting ready for her second throw.

"Forty-two feet," a man said. He held a measuring tape from the white line in front of Sundi to the skillet in the distance.

Josh Whatley leaned against the end of a picnic table.

"Skillet-throwing helps?" I asked.

"Hey." Josh stood up, unfolded his arms, straightened

his belt buckle, and looked down at me from under his bangs. "You win?"

"Yeah." I was beaming, couldn't help it. My Bantam cock took first place in the Poultry Division. I even thought about telling Josh to get his daddy's truck washed up and ready for the no-Jesus parade. I could be the next sweetheart. But I glanced at Sundi. She had untied the spaghetti straps on her top, leaving the elastic band to hold it up and giving her shoulders freedom to move. She pounded her hands on a flour-covered board. Her thin, blond hair, plastered stiff with Aqua Net hair spray, matted in the humid twilight like cotton candy spun around a stick. Sending her lamb to be slaughtered seemed to smash all the air out of the marshmallow girl. She looked stale, like a dried-out version of her real self.

"I just feel so awful for her," I said.

Josh pulled me in front of him, placing both his hands around my waist and resting his chin on top of my head. I went stiff as a wooden nutcracker. But inside, my heart danced.

"She'll be all right." Josh and Sundi were county kids from the same small community outside of Big Wells. They seemed to understand each other like brother and sister. "We've seen farm animals born and butchered since we were little."

We watched Sundi dust the excess flour from her hands and get ready for her last throw. "She knows market animals sometimes get pegged for market."

I stared across the field to the Prosper Lake Bridge in the distance. "But it rattles your cage when you lose someone you love. Especially when it's sudden. And unnecessary."

I stepped out from Josh's touch. Good grief. Here I was at the skillet-throwing contest at the county fair, and I was getting philosophical about my own personal loss issues. I'd never really had a boy *friend* before, and I felt strangely like I could talk to him, like I wanted to talk to him, like talking to Maribel. But he wasn't Maribel. He was a broad-shouldered, suntanned cowboy in tight jeans and a tight T-shirt. The closer he drew me in, the further I was off the firm ground of good sense. Sweet boys are like candy, Momma says. They're best kept out of arms' reach or a girl will wind up wanting a little every hour of the day.

Sundi grabbed another black iron skillet, twirling the handle with one floured hand. She got behind the white line and swung the skillet back and forth, brushing the open side against her leg. She stepped back a few feet, aiming the skillet out in front of her like a bowler with a ball. Then she took off. One step, another step, a third step, and she swung the skillet underhanded into the field. It split into black iron chunks when it hit the grass.

"Fifty-six feet!" the man with the tape measure hollered. "A new Prosper County Fair record."

Josh and I clapped with the rest of the crowd. Sundi beat and rubbed her hands against her starched Wrangler jeans, getting rid of some of the flour. She stomped our way.

She stopped in front of Josh and me with her hands on her hips. Her mascara was gone except for the blue watercolor discs underneath her lower eyelashes. "Let's go ride the Wicked Windmill."

"Charles Dickens won first place." Josh gestured at me.

For a second, Sundi softened. "That's great, Austin." Then she dried back up. "Am I going to have to ride the Wicked Windmill by myself?"

Josh and I followed Sundi as she marched through the fair's midway, making a beeline toward the Wicked Windmill. She all but shoved one tattooed carnie when he stepped in front of her and asked if he could guess her weight. The ping-ding of winning bells and the flashing neon carnival lit up the fairgrounds, lit up the night. Lit up everything but Sundi.

We got in the Wicked Windmill line behind her.

"Maribel's bringing her ice cream by my house later. After this ride, maybe you both could come over." As weak as that was, I thought getting Sundi away from the fairgrounds would be helpful. Moving on to the next thing was what I knew. I didn't know what to say. I couldn't tell her the truth. Loss isn't something you get over; it's something you get through.

"She just needs time to vent," Josh whispered in my ear, scorching the entire right side of my body.

Sundi reached into her pocket and pulled out a folded check. "I tried to give it back," she sniffled.

The line we were in snaked around. I watched dizzily as

the scream-filled cages spun on the end of each arm of the Wicked Windmill. The operator, a braless woman in a dirty tank top, jerked the controls with one hand and fed herself a turkey leg with the other. No way was I getting on that ride.

"It's two to a cage." I backed a couple steps out of the line. "Why don't you both ride together."

Josh grinned. The carnival lights flickered in his green eyes. Sundi reached her hand out and rubbed my arm. I saw her soft heart coming back through her face.

"Holy crap, Austin Gray!" Dean Ottmer spit a sunflower seed. He'd gotten in line behind us. "How much more lame can you get?"

Dean-O was back-o. An ever-present hitch in my giddyup. I took a deep breath and blew out a big "I'm ignoring you, you don't exist" sigh. Maybe it was Charles Dickens's blue-ribbon win or Sundi's broken heart, years of praying the problem or maybe just exhaustion, but Dean Ottmer didn't even pierce my skin this time. For the first time ever, he didn't matter much to me. But he did matter to Sundi. She wanted to save something.

"Shut your smart mouth, Dean." Sundi puffed up and faced him. Her girls heaved up and down.

Dean had a mouthful of sunflower seeds, which he spit like rapid gunfire onto the fairground. Dean smiled big to his gang. He made sure they were all looking.

"Sundi had a little lamb. Its fleece was white as snow." Dean mimicked some gang sign and tried to rhyme like the white rapper he wasn't. "My daddy bought him at the fair. On the grill Sundi's lamb will go."

Sundi pulled the check out of her pocket. This time she unfolded it. OTTMER FORD, INC. spelled out in black capital letters in the left corner of the check. Frank Ottmer had bought her lamb and sent it to slaughter—knowing full well she intended to keep it.

"Do you hear the lambs, Sundi?" Dean dug deep into his recollection of late-night movies and attempted Anthony Hopkins. Dean's version of *Silence of the Lambs* was less eerie and more empty. Lewis Fortenberry was right. Dean Ottmer was just a big nothing with no original thoughts behind that mouth. But his intimidated friends kept propping him up with their laughter, so Dean went full out. Sucking all the life out of his spotlight. A real one-man show.

"I do wish we could chat longer, but I'm having an old friend for dinner."

Sundi ripped her three-thousand-dollar check into pieces, staring at Dean and inching closer to him.

"Time to go, Sundi," Josh said. He tried pulling her out of line.

Sundi didn't pull easily. She had older brothers. Nothing male intimidated her. "Tell your daddy to keep his money." She tossed the torn check in the air like confetti.

Dean was too caught up in his own performance to notice Sundi had eased within arm's length of him. He went one Hannibal Lecter quote too many.

"I'll eat the lamb's liver with some fava beans and a nice Chianti."

Sundi pulled back her floured right fist and, faster than a spinning arm of the Wicked Windmill, the marshmallow girl flattened Dean Ottmer's nose. Punched it like pie dough. Dean grabbed his face, then bent over, dripping blood and drooling spit and sunflower seeds. Sundi waited on Dean to straighten up. She never once batted what was left of her blue-coated eyelashes.

"Get up or shut up."

Dean chose to shut up. His supposed friends stood steps away from him with their arms folded at their waists, leaving him alone in the spotlight he so loved.

I had played with marshmallows—pressing one onto the end of each finger, mashing them down just to watch them spring back up. They were soft but tough, resilient. No matter the pressure or poking, they almost always returned to their original shape.

Sundi left Dean on all fours and smiled at me. "Maybe we could go to your house." A softness returned to her face. She sucked in her gut and slipped a tube of pink gloss from her jeans pocket, globbing some over her lips. "A little ice cream sounds good."

"You need some help, Dean?" Josh offered because Dean's good friends left him bent over and bleeding. Dean stuck his middle finger up—his personal testimony that he was just fine and dandy.

Sundi never looked back.

For me, it was a rock star moment. Sundi Knutt—the marshmallow girl, the sweetheart—in the weepy throws of despair pounding my archenemy into silence. But it was her moment, not mine. Sundi stood up; I didn't.

We left the fairgrounds, but I learned something from Sundi that being a sweetheart in the no-Jesus parade couldn't provide. Sundi traveled light; she didn't tote around a load of loss. She could throw away or throw down. Either way, she put stuff behind her. She didn't get her confidence from a prize lamb, a mound of cleavage, or a hood ride in the no-Jesus parade. Her confidence came from facing the losses and losers, not being a hood ornament. That's the strength of a marshmallow sweetheart.

The time had come for me to cowgirl up and stand firm in my own boots.

one more compromise

"**I** can't shoot Bambi!" I repeatedly told Maribel.

My chances of becoming a hood ornament in the No-Jesus Christmas Parade now rested on adding sport hunting to my FFA Sweetheart résumé. Charles Dickens's first-place finish wasn't enough. Sundi had a deer hunting license, too.

"Think of it as venison." Maribel wrapped a set of dinner plates in white wedding paper. July was a big month for the bridal registry at Gray's True Value. "Deer meat is a delicacy in fine dining."

"Do you not see the tragic irony in killing Rudolph to get into the Christmas parade?" I rolled two crystal goblets in bubble pack.

"Austin, Rudolph is a reindeer. No chef serves reindeer." Maribel was indignant, like I should've known the difference between Bambi meat and Rudolph meat.

It just seemed like rocky logic to me. Maribel could draw a line between pet and protein. So could Sundi. She apparently saw nothing conflicting in the grief over the Ottmers having her lamb for dinner and the pride in bagging a trophy buck. I wished for Sundi's bold confidence: the kind that allows a girl to cry over one animal's slaughter, daub on a little lip shine, and shoot another. And not worry about being viewed as crazy. No one thought Sundi Knutt was unstable.

Mayor Nesmith swung open the front door of the store and charged down the center aisle. He had on khaki shorts, a red T-shirt with the American flag on the front, and a baseball cap. The hairy mayor looked like a patriotic dress-up teddy bear. Charles Dickens sailed off his perch, following Nesmith to the wrap counter in the middle of the store.

"Where's Jeannie?" Nesmith demanded.

Charles Dickens let out a "HAAAAAWK." I picked him up and rubbed his wattle. "She's out back with a delivery truck."

"Well, I want the biggest butcher knife you've got." He eyeballed my rooster.

"HAAAAWK!" Charles Dickens belted out another alarm.

I heard Momma's boots hit the wooden floor at the back of the store. Charles Dickens had become her watchdog. She recognized his "HAAAWK" as a sign of trouble.

"What is it, Victor?" Momma dabbed the sweat off her forehead and chest with one of Glammy's old lace handkerchiefs. Momma was as much of an incongruity as Sundi. Momma wore boots, jeans, and black sleeveless shirts that drew attention to her muscular arms. But she was all woman, with her lace handkerchiefs and jaw-dropping curves.

128

Nesmith, as he did every time, forgot what he came in for. "Well? What is it, Victor?" Momma repeated.

"He wants the biggest butcher knife you've got." Maribel helped Nesmith out.

"The breast one, I mean the best one you've got," he stammered, trying to take his eyes off her shirt buttons. "One that will cut"—he cupped his hands and held them out—"big watermelons." Nesmith drew up the corners of his mouth like the Grinch. "I'm taking the party barge out on the lake tonight for the Fourth of July fireworks show."

Momma escorted Nesmith to the knife display.

"Kiwi man." Maribel wound a yarn string into a bow.

"Kiwi man?"

"That's what he is," Maribel continued, "kiwi man—hairy on the outside, slimy on the inside."

We laughed and Charles Dickens clucked. Nesmith stood behind the checkout counter, continuing to yap at Momma. She let him rattle on, flat ignoring him, while she rang up his machete of a butcher knife.

"No, thanks. I stay away from the lake." Momma handed him his credit card receipt to sign.

I put Charles Dickens down when Momma said "lake." She avoided the lake like she avoided talking on Christmas Eves.

"You gotta move on sometime," Nesmith the kiwi man begged.

I pretended to tie a bow on an already wrapped wedding gift.

129

"I have moved on." Momma sounded irritated. "Just not with married men and not with Prosper Lake."

I twisted the yarn bow around and around my index finger. Momma, in her own way, had moved on since Daddy's death. But not like Sundi, who let all the hurt out and then left it behind. A pet lamb is one thing; a husband, a father is another. Momma moved on, but she packed up and carried a suitcase full of loss for the trip.

Nesmith left the store swinging the sack with his new knife in it by his leg.

"He has an unhealthy lack of respect for kitchen utensils," Maribel said.

"If you ask me"—I carried Charles Dickens back to his storefront perch—"he has an unhealthy respect for everything." I turned the knob on the gumball machine, letting the scratch fill my palm. Charles Dickens ate out of my hand while I watched Big Wells begin to celebrate Independence Day.

American flags proudly hanging in front of the shops around the square blew in the hot breath of summer. A wooden Uncle Sam patriotically painted with red, white, and blue stripes saluted the customers going in and out of Wanda's Antique Mall. Trucks pulling ski boats, and cars loaded with teenagers and coolers, zipped through downtown on their way to Prosper Lake. Another Fourth of July— heck, another summer—and I was dry-docked in downtown Big Wells. Momma couldn't stand the thought of me going to the lake. She had a personal grudge against it. For her,

Prosper Lake would always be the dark water that took Daddy away from us.

An old El Camino with new chrome rims screeched to a parallel stop in front of the store. According to the duck hunting bumper sticker on the back window, *If it flies, it dies*.

"Stay still, buddy," I warned Charles Dickens as Sundi Knutt, suntanned and perky, hopped out of her car. I met her outside on the sidewalk.

"Hey." Sundi flip-flopped in front of me. She had on a yellow-check bikini modestly hidden under cutoff blue jean shorts and an exhausted-looking tube top, stretched to the max and sagging. She hooked her thumbs under the elastic band—tug, tug, pop, and her girls were back, front and center.

"Going to the lake?"

"*We* are going to the lake," Sundi clarified. "Josh will be there." She giggled and looked over the top of her aviator sunglasses.

Josh and I had talked a few times on the phone since the county fair. Following Momma's advice about keeping candy out of reach was getting harder to do.

"Everyone else in FFA will be there, too."

Through the glass storefront, I saw Maribel wrapping the last few wedding gifts. Momma swept the center aisle. I felt an ache in my gut. "I can't go."

"Isn't the store closing early?" Sundi's voice lifted a little. She put her hand over her tube-topped heart like she took my not going with her to the lake personally.

"It's not that."

Momma stopped her sweeping. She waved at Sundi.

"She doesn't let me go boating or swim at the lake," I explained, hoping not to go into the details of why. Although I was sure Sundi, like the rest of the tri-county area, knew Momma's reasons.

"Perfect!" Sundi seemed relieved. "We won't be swimming or boating." She opened the front door of Gray's True Value. "We hang out on a hillside by Old Cypress Creek where we watch fireworks and fish." Sundi and I stepped into the store. "Maribel can come, too."

FFA and fishing, I thought to myself. Fishing could be a way around the deer hunting thing. Catch and release. Just reel 'em in, then throw 'em back into the water. No messy cleanup. No guilty conscience. This I could do.

"Sundi, you look like you're headed to the lake," Momma said, sweeping dirt into a dustpan.

"Not exactly." Sundi wiggled her toes in her flip-flops and hung her sunglasses on the middle of her tube top. "I came to see if Austin, and Maribel if she wants to"—Sundi waved at Maribel—"could go with us to watch the fireworks."

"Who's us?" Momma propped the broom in the corner by the register.

"Me, Josh, Ricky, some other kids from FFA. We watch the fireworks from a hillside by Old Cypress Creek."

"By the bridge?" Momma asked. Maribel stopped wrapping.

"We turn off before the bridge." Sundi's blue eyes

widened as if she realized she had suddenly stepped on a snake. "We turn off way before the bridge. We don't go near the bridge."

Momma stared at me. I shifted my eyes to Maribel.

"I'm out." Maribel shrugged her shoulders like she was sorry but couldn't help it. "*La familia.* Mamanita and I are cooking tonight. Some of her *pico* customers want my Mango Kick ice cream."

Sundi stuck out a shiny-pink bottom lip. "That just leaves you, Austin."

Momma stood with her feet apart, hands shoved in her back pockets. She inventoried Sundi—scrolling from her flip-flops to the string bikini tied around her neck and hidden under the tube top.

"I promise I won't get in a boat or swim." I interrupted Momma's mental inventory before she took too much note of Sundi's tube top. I was desperate to go. "A lot of the FFA club will be there." She liked the FFA group, thought they were hardworking. And she knew how important it was to me to be a real member of their crowd.

Momma pulled her hands from her pockets and ran them through the spikes in her hair. "Stay out of the lake. No going out on boats or Jet Skis. No swimming."

A part of me was in shock. The other parts hugged her with both arms. Sundi, with no intentions of being left out of a hugfest, pressed against us.

"And be home *immediately* after the fireworks," Momma added.

It took all the courage Momma had to allow me to go with Sundi. Courage to put aside her fears and allow me to stretch my friendships and freedoms a little. And it took courage for her to trust me, especially after the disaster at Nesmith's barbecue. I didn't want to do anything to set her back.

The passenger-side door to Sundi's El Camino squeaked when I opened it to hop in. "Run me by my house so I can change out of my work clothes."

The car only had a radio, so Sundi had installed a CD player mounted under the ashtray. She put in Kenny Chesney and turned up the volume. Two tracks in, we turned onto Camellia Heights.

"You'll need your bathing suit, Austin," Sundi said as I slid out the door.

I stopped with one foot on the ground, the other still in the car. I whipped my head around in disbelief. She had heard my Momma. She knew full well what my limits were.

"I know, I know," she said over Kenny Chesney. "No boating, no swimming. Fireworks and fishing is all. I promise." She smiled through her eyes. "Just get your swimsuit on."

There was such honesty in her blue eyes. Such honesty I wanted to trust. Such honesty I decided to chance to trust.

I took off my clothes and left them in a pile on the floor of my room. I stepped into my swimsuit, the turquoise one-piece with the padded bra liner. I slipped into my favorite denim mini and a tank top, brushed my hair into a ponytail, and pulled on my boots. *No boating, no swimming,* I reminded myself. Then I adjusted the swimsuit straps under the tank and headed outside to Sundi and Kenny Chesney and Josh and the FFA and fishing and Fourth of July fireworks and the dark water of Prosper Lake.

15

grappling

Sundi's head was almost totally submerged underwater. Only her face—mouth, nose, and eyes—floated on top of Old Cypress Creek. I watched from the bank as her face bobbed in the coffee-colored water. She went under twenty, maybe thirty seconds, forever it seemed. Then, in a fountain of mad splashes, Sundi burst through the surface with one arm crammed into the mouth and through the gills of what weighed in as a thirty-eight-pound catfish.

Grappling. Bare-handed fishing.

Sundi's spotters, Ricky and another boy in the creek with her, wrapped their arms around the catfish as if they were toting a log. Sundi pulled her arm free. The kids around us, the ones kicked back in lawn chairs and truck beds, applauded and whooped.

"Your turn." Josh smiled.

When I was little, Daddy used to tuck me in at night with what he called redneck fairy tales. My favorite was the one about the giant blue catfish, Mr. Malvo Whiskers, who lurked in a dark hole near the bank and under the shallow water of Prosper Lake. He protected the eggs laid by the female, his catfish wife. *"Mr. Malvo Whiskers wouldn't leave the egg babies, not even to eat,"* Daddy whispered. *"He was so hungry, he'd snap at anything moving in front of his hole."* Daddy wiggled his fingers, tapping them across my arm, and pinched me.

Josh squeezed the tops of my arms. "You ready?"

Sundi sloshed through the creek and up the bank toward us. Her girls swinging with every cumbersome step. No more than a few hundred yards behind her, Old Cypress Creek emptied into Prosper Lake. Ski boats raced across the lake and under the bridge.

"I'm not exactly dressed for grappling." I pointed at my boots.

Sundi dripped in front of Josh and me. She carried a neoprene glove in one hand and a pair of river sandals, the ones with the Velcro straps, in the other. "Here you go." She handed the gear to me.

"One sunny day," Daddy said, *"a little girl wandered into the muddy water near Mr. Malvo Whiskers' precious, protected nest."* Daddy pulled the covers around my neck. *"The kids in the village had made fun of her because she didn't have a special job. She wasn't one of the kids who made the tea sweet, and she wasn't one of the kids who painted the village wooden yard art."* Daddy kissed my forehead. *"There was nothing special about her, she thought, so she set out to become more special than any other kid in the village."*

"You know," I stalled, "my idea of fishing includes, and this may sound crazy, a rod and reel and a bunch of fat worms."

Sundi and Josh laughed. Then Josh scooped me up with both arms and Sundi tugged my boots off. She strapped her Velcro river shoes to my feet. I decided to go limp. I just hung there in Josh's arms, looking upside down into the sunset, praying for a sudden rainstorm, and thinking about Mr. Malvo Whiskers.

"The little girl knew that if she could catch the great blue catfish, her entire village would eat for a year. She would become the village princess. Everyone would treat her like royalty. That would make her special." Daddy smoothed the top of my hair. "So the little girl bravely reached under the water, sliding her hand across the slimy mud and feeling around for a hole. Her hand passed over a cool spot, a hole with sandy sides—Mr. Malvo Whiskers' precious, protected nest."

Josh flipped me to my feet. The breeze coming off the creek carried the foul, wet odor of a day-old bucket of minnows. Fishing. That's what we'd told Momma.

The FFA group chanted, "Austin, Austin, Austin," from their creekside amphitheater. I counted sweetheart votes. If I could somehow pull this grappling thing off, I would definitely be the FFA hood ornament in the no-Jesus parade. The sweetheart of Prosper County.

As much as I knew Momma would split a seam, I just couldn't find it in me to stop. Too much momentum in the wrong direction. Technically, grappling was fishing. I was sure the Indians had done it as a way of life.

I pulled my tank top off over my head and shimmied out

of my denim mini. From the corner of my eye, I caught Josh staring. Goose bumps raced across my arms and legs; everything shriveled. Thank God for swimsuits with padded bra liners.

Josh, Sundi, and I inched beside an old boat ramp and floated near the bank in shoulder-high water.

"Feel under the water, on the bottom and along the bank, for a hole," Josh said. "Stay away from grassy areas and clumps of sticks or brush. That's where the cottonmouths, the water moccasins are."

I felt sick. The tepid creek water had an algae film on top and a musty fish smell. I kept my lips pinched together and took short, quick breaths through my nose. The creek bed and bank were either slimy mud slicks or knobby-knuckled tree roots. I couldn't see a thing below the surface. Not the snapping turtles, not the beavers, not the snakes. But I eased further along, holding cypress tree roots on the side of the creek bank with one hand and blindly feeling across the red, slick mud for holes with the other.

We had floated downstream almost to the mouth of Old Cypress Creek. The FFA boys and girls on the bank were barely in yelling distance. The bridge across Prosper Lake, the bridge Daddy drove off of, was almost close enough to swim to. The sun was setting and tree stumps stuck up above the lake like gravestones. Cypress trees along the water's edge eclipsed the last ray of sunshine.

The darkness and the muddy water closed in around

me. I thought I saw the ghostly silhouette of a man float like a phantom among the cypress.

I turned away.

Josh was close enough to reach.

I stole another glance into the trees. Not really sure I wanted to look. The figure was there again, then gone. Like some discarded scarecrow blown about in the breeze.

"I've got one in a log!" Sundi yelled.

She scared me so, I grabbed at the creek sides. My hands sunk deep into the claylike mud, cold between my fingers.

Sundi stood in the black water and motioned for Josh and me. "This end is blocked. He can't get out." Sundi pressed her shins onto one end of the log.

"You don't have to do this." Josh tugged at the muddy glove on my right hand. "Most girls wouldn't have made it as far as you have. Everyone thinks they'll do it until it's time to stick their hand in a hole."

"I'm not ready to quit."

Daddy finished his redneck fairy tale. "The little girl wiggled her fingers under the water in front of Mr. Malvo Whiskers' precious, protected nest. A long, great blue catfish whisker brushed across her arm." Daddy drew his finger slowly down my blanket. "Then Mr. Malvo Whiskers swallowed her arm, all the way up to her shoulder, in his mouth." Daddy ran his arm under my pillow and pulled me closer to him. "Just as Mr. Malvo Whiskers was about to have a little girl for lunch, her daddy, the little girl's daddy, pulled them both out of the water." I always sleepily mumbled Yee-haw for daddies on that part. "Even though her daddy saved her, the lit-

tle girl complained that now she would never ever be special. The daddy couldn't believe his ears. His little girl didn't think she was special." Daddy squeezed me good-night. "Little girl of mine," he said, "any kid can make the tea sweet and any kid can paint the village yard art. Special is something one of a kind. The only one. And only you can be my little girl."

For me, special would always be something drowned in Prosper Lake. I stretched my fingers, spreading my gloved hand wide, then made a fist.

"When the fish bites . . ." Josh had one arm around my shoulders and demonstrated with the other. "Don't jerk back. Ram your fist through his gills, then hold both your wrists like you've got him in a kind of headlock." Josh's eyes got big and he cocked a grin. "Your arm is gonna be in his mouth. Hold tight and pull back and up." Josh moved behind me, squeezing his fingers around my hips. "He'll suck you under, but I won't let you drown."

"You can do it, Austin." Sundi reached under the water and held the log steady. "Take deep breaths."

I slowly lowered myself, sinking into the water, sticking my gloved hand into the log. I wiggled my fingers. Nothing happened. I stood back up.

"I think it's gone," I said, hoping that was good enough.

"Deeper, Austin." Sundi took grappling seriously. Her eyes darkened to sapphire, and the softness in her voice sharpened. "Past your elbows. Both arms in the log."

Long shadows spread across the lake as the sun went down. Boat lights and pier lights flickered on. I sank again, reaching deeper into the hollow log and wiggling my fingers. My face dipped in the water. I shot up.

Josh patted my hips with both hands. "You don't have to try again. It's getting dark."

"I'm not quitting." My life was all about grappling, struggling in particular with the what-would-have-beens had my daddy not driven off the Prosper Lake Bridge. Grappling for catfish was simply a way for me to take something out of the water and make a new name for myself. Less Austin Gray had a daddy who drowned in Prosper Lake and more Austin Gray had a blue-ribbon-winning rooster and could catch a catfish with her bare hands.

Furthermore, I could fill FFA Sweetheart characteristic number two, sport hunting, without ever firing a shot.

Catching the fish was something I had to do.

"Take a breath and go under, Austin," Sundi encouraged. "Reach into the log as deep as you can."

If marshmallow girl could do it, so could I. I bounced three times in the water, took a deep breath, held it, and went under. I stuck both arms, nearly to my shoulders, into the log. Quick and hard, the catfish snapped onto my left hand like a bulldog. I jerked back, sucking in a mouthful of lake water. The thing yanked my hand and gulped my arm halfway to the elbow. My shoulders slammed against the log. I felt Josh gripping my hips, but he didn't know I was out of breath. I was choking and in a tug-of-war with the catfish for my left arm. My fingers found his gills. I punched my gloved hand through his grill plate and clasped it with my right hand. I held on, wrestling to pull out the catfish and fighting to come up for air.

Josh wrapped both his arms around my waist and pulled me back. I budged and the catfish's teeth raked like sandpaper over my forearm. I tightened my locked arms and pushed my feet onto the floor of Old Cypress Creek. Both feet pressed through the slimy mud. I sank shin-deep.

Oh, God! I prayed the problem. *I'm drowning in Prosper Lake.*

Josh pulled and tugged, but I could feel him slipping on the creek bed.

The inside of the catfish was bony and cold. My head felt light.

Another arm, not Josh's, clamped around my rib cage and jerked me backward. The catfish charged forward through the log, and I broke through the water. Gasping. Coughing. Spitting up.

"Let go now," someone told me.

Josh held tightly to my waist. Sundi hugged the tail of the blue cat to keep it from slapping around.

I was dizzy and puking lake water, but I was alert enough to see Lafitte Boudreaux pulling my bloody arm out of the mouth of an enormous and ugly catfish.

"We gotta get Miss Aus'in out dis water and off the bank," he hollered. "Gators on the move at dusk. They'll be tastin' blood."

Truck headlights beamed across the creek, finding us near the bank. Sundi looked ghost white in her bikini. She stood frozen and holding on to the catfish. For the first time ever, I saw fear in her big blue eyes. Lafitte Boudreaux wrangled the catfish, wrapping both arms over and around it.

"Ya let go dat tail now," he told Sundi. "And get outta dis water."

She released the catfish's tail. It slapped the water and rolled over, rolling Lafitte Boudreaux onto his back and under. He surfaced, soaking wet, climbing the cypress tree roots and pulling himself up.

Josh pitched me onto the bank. I landed on my stomach and threw up the last of the muddy, fishy water. He scrambled out behind me. Rising up on all fours, I caught sight of my left arm in the truck's headlights. Down my forearm, from my elbow to the back of my hand, an inch-wide bloody stripe burned from dirt and grass and creek water.

"Ya'll okay? Ya'll need some help?" a voice hollered from behind the truck lights on the opposite side of the creek. It sounded like Ricky.

Panting, Lafitte Boudreaux warned Josh. "You can get on back in dat water if you wahns. But Miss Aus'in comin' wid me." He breathed heavily. "Ah ain't leavin' her. Ah ain't leavin' Miss Aus'in." He helped me to my feet. "Ya's comin' wid me."

Josh and Sundi looked at Lafitte Boudreaux gripping my arm, then at each other.

"We're okay," Josh hollered back across the creek. "We're going with Austin's"—Josh stared at Lafitte Boudreaux—"friend. Give us two hours, then call for help if you haven't heard from us."

Josh took off his river sandals and handed them to Sundi. She was barefoot. "We need to go with the old man," he said.

Sundi strapped on the sandals. "Austin, can you walk?" she asked.

"Yeah." I spit creek grit onto the ground.

Lafitte Boudreaux hung on to my right arm, guiding me as we set out through the thicket.

"I'll be okay, Mr. Boudreaux," I told him over and over. But he wouldn't let go. I felt him squeeze his hand around my arm every few seconds, like he was making sure I was still there. Making sure some voodoo haint in the darkness hadn't sucked the breath from me. Like a possessed man, the old Creole trudged toward his yellow tree house flickering through the thicket, up the hill, in and out of sight.

like father, like daughter

Tires spinning gravel skidded to a stop in front of the bygone station. In the back, where we were, Lafitte Boudreaux had rolled up the plastic sides of his apartment-porch. A warm summer breeze stirred his jazz-postered ceiling. Sundi, clutching a bath towel around her bare shoulders, rested on the couch where Charles Dickens's box had been last Christmas. Josh stood beside the sink basin, watching Lafitte Boudreaux swab the skinless strip down my forearm. Fireworks popped and whistled, sprinkling the tree-tops with bright sparks.

We heard the swishing of someone running through the dry grass below the tree house. Boots hit the plank steps. *Click-clack, click-clack, click-clack.* Momma threw open the screen door.

"My God, Austin!" Momma went stark white when she saw my bloody arm stretched across the sink.

"She all right now, she all right." Lafitte Boudreaux tried to be reassuring. He didn't bother giving her any details over the phone when he called her to come get me. "We ain't amputatin' yet."

Momma leaned over the sink and stared at my arm. "How?" She shook her head, side to side, in disbelief. "What did this to you?"

"Mr. Malvo Whiskers," I said, numb and dumb from the pain.

She squinted at me like she was trying to bring a ghost into focus. As if saying "Mr. Malvo Whiskers" conjured up some of Lafitte Boudreaux's voodoo and brought my dead daddy to life.

"Noodlin's what Ah calls it." Mr. Boudreaux blew air over my arm as he dripped hydrogen peroxide over the gash.

It stung like he'd jabbed me with a hot needle. I clenched my teeth and tried not to cry.

"Miss Aus'in got hold of some big cat." Lafitte Boudreaux never took his eyes off my arm, never looked at Momma. "Sixty, seventy pound maybe."

"You tried to *grapple*?" She turned on Sundi. "Is that your idea of fishing?"

Sundi sat motionless. Her blond hair stuck in mats to her head. Like me, she probably preferred a hot bath instead of my momma's wrath.

"I wasn't going to let her drown." Josh tried to shoulder Momma's blame. "We've never had this kind of trouble before."

"And what kind is that?" Momma snapped. "The kind

of trouble that occurs when poor judgment takes the place of good sense? The kind that says we'll keep sticking our hands in an underwater hole until a beaver gnaws off an arm or a turtle nips off a finger or a water moccasin loads some kid up with venom?" Momma's voice got louder. Josh respectfully kept his eyes on her; Sundi sniffled on the couch. "Or until some pissed-off catfish holds my daughter underwater until she drowns?" She gave Josh a sharp poke in his chest with her index finger. "You've got better sense than that."

"Josh tried to talk me out of it, Momma." I winced as the hydrogen peroxide bubbled and foamed in the bloody strip on the back of my hand. Mr. Boudreaux wound gauze around my arm. "Blame me," I finished. "I wanted to do it. I wasn't quitting till I got one."

Momma stared a hole through me as Lafitte Boudreaux wrapped the last of the bandage. "Well, it looks like it got you. You know . . ." Momma rubbed a gauze scrap between her fingers. "I thought you'd use better judgment, Austin. But you're just getting more like your father every day."

Mr. Boudreaux slowly tightened the cap on the peroxide bottle. Josh pretended to read the blues and rockabilly posters covering the ceiling. Sundi soaked up the tears from her suntanned cheeks with a corner of the towel. No one uttered a word.

I closed my eyes, damming up my own tears. The peroxide in my bloody arm didn't sting half as bad as Momma's words. I hated that I hurt her, but I hated more that she chose this time and place to bring up my daddy. I didn't know whether to apologize or call her out. So I did what I had learned to do: I wiped my eyes and moved on.

Josh, Sundi, and I loaded into Momma's Jeep.

Lafitte Boudreaux stood alone on the trail beside the old storefront. No one had really thanked him. I raised my good arm and gave a slight wave. He dropped his head and disappeared down the trail.

Momma spun around in the gravel, catching traction on the blacktop road. Possum Trot. The same road Sundi took to the creek was the same road that led to Lafitte Boudreaux's house. I hadn't recognized Possum Trot as the road Momma and I had taken last Christmas Eve.

Momma drove the Jeep off Possum Trot and down to the creek where several of the FFA kids waited, despite the fireworks over Prosper Lake being long gone.

"I'm sorry for your grief," Josh told Momma as he climbed out. "For the added grief our taking Austin to the creek has caused you." Momma didn't respond, didn't even look at him.

But I did. I saw in Josh's face that he got it. That Momma's anger was more about Momma and my daddy than him and grappling.

I could hardly face him. Josh was just so genuine. And I hated that the Gray family "unspeakable" had left him feeling guilty and confused, too.

Sundi reached into the front seat and hugged me. "I'll check on you later."

Momma drove the Jeep back onto Possum Trot, speeding over the potholed road to the highway.

"Just what exactly does that mean?" I couldn't possibly be in more physical pain, so I found the courage to confront her.

"Does what mean?" She didn't recall her own slam.

"The crack about my getting more like my father every day."

Momma pulled to a stop at the intersection of Possum Trot and the highway.

"What point were you trying to make?" I demanded.

Momma dropped the gearshift into low. She whipped her head around and leaned over the console. "You're becoming reckless, Austin." She lasered me with her hot, black eyes. I pushed my shoulders hard against the seat, pulling back from her glare. "You shave off the sharp edges of truth, making something gray out of something that is black and white. For example, Nesmith's barbecue. Now you've chanced danger by grappling. I have no problem with you scheming your way into the Christmas parade. Have I not been supportive? But I do have a problem when you submit to compromising your values and your life, for God's sake, for a sweetheart dream." She slinked back into her seat, staring through the windshield. "You have to keep your head in the game. Think about all the consequences, long and hard, before flying off and doing something. Otherwise, you'll wind up exactly like your father."

"And just how is that?" I pushed her. "How is that, Momma?"

"You know where his choices took him. We deal with that every day. Remember?"

"Actually, I don't remember." I felt a tingling in my chest, the place where tears start. "I remember church ladies with hams and Velveeta casseroles and old people pressing their hollow, gummy mouths against my cheeks." I wiped tears on my gauze-covered arm. "I remember feeling sick from the moldy smell of potted plants lined up in front of the fireplace, and whispers. I remember Glammy making me write down everyone's name and the food they brought on a yellow legal pad. She was mad because I didn't know how to write in cursive. I had to print." I yelled, "I was only in third grade. Third grade! I didn't know cursive, I didn't know all those people in my house, and I didn't know what happened to my daddy! I still don't. You never talk about it. We don't have conversations. And we don't have Christmas! We can't even have Christmas!"

Momma floored the Jeep, squealing onto the highway away from the lights of Big Wells. She sped toward the Prosper Lake Bridge. She was bawling, gushing tears and heaving voiced sobs that sounded eerily like deranged laughter.

I may have pushed her too far. Watching her break, I realized that Momma hadn't just been trying to protect me. She'd been protecting herself.

The July night was both bright and dark, a star-filled

indigo. We topped the hill. Waiting below, a narrow two-lane bridge stretched across Prosper Lake. The Jeep picked up speed.

"Slow down!" I screamed at Momma. She gripped the wheel with both hands and fought to see the road through her tears. The Jeep rolled on, faster and faster, to the bottom of the hill and the Prosper Lake Bridge.

The bridge came closer into view. "Stop! Slow down!" I yelled again.

Momma punched the clutch with her foot, threw the gearshift into neutral. The Jeep jerked and whined as the engine stopped racing. Momma steered the Jeep away from the bridge, off the road, down a makeshift mud slick boat ramp, and into Prosper Lake. The Jeep slid to a stop, water sloshing halfway up the tires. Momma opened the door and stepped into the lake.

"He took too many chances, Austin!" She kicked around in the water. Crying and kicking. Finally, Momma put her hands in her back pockets and stared up at the bridge. "His *muscle car* he called it. Always driving too fast. You heard him before you saw him." She half laughed, part hysteria, part heart cry. "Either blaring Journey or revving the engine. He bought that car, used, in high school and would not give it up."

Momma may have been just talking to the darkness or to herself, but I had a right to the story.

"I remember that car. Black with wide, white stripes on the hood." I waded around the Jeep. Momma was finally talking and to whom didn't matter. I wasn't going to miss any chance to hear about my daddy.

She sat down in the shallow water and pulled her knees to her chest. I'm not sure she knew she was in the lake. "After we married, we took road trips in that thing. Driving around the hill country outside of Austin in the hot summer in a gas guzzler with no air-conditioning. But he loved it. The car, the road trips, the Texas hill country." She ran her hand through the water, letting it pass through her fingers. "You're stubborn like him. That's why I didn't argue when you said you wanted a chicken for Christmas. I knew you wouldn't let it go, and if you did, what came next would be worse." She tossed her head back and stared at the stars. "Just like I let him name you Austin, because I was afraid he'd pick something else like Mustang or Chevelle." She sobbed and laughed in a kind of long overdue mourning requiem. Her tears flowed into Prosper Lake.

For the first time, I heard how lonesome sounds and saw how deeply she missed him.

I waded, ankle deep, beside her.

"He was delivering a special-order pellet gun to someone on the other side of the lake. It was Christmas Eve and a little boy's Santa Claus gift came late to the store." She looked up at me. "It gave him an excuse to hot-rod his car. They said he went airborne at the top of the hill." We looked back at the highway, to the hilltop leading up to the bridge. "The skid marks showed that he landed on the rain-slick road, then skidded out of control onto the bridge and over.

The skid marks showed he fought to right the car but over-corrected." Momma breathed a deep, ragged breath. "Had it not been raining, he might have straightened it out."

I knelt down in the water, holding up my gauzed arm. I made her look at me. Look me in the face.

"But he didn't," Momma said. "And Lafitte Boudreaux pulled you out of the water tonight, Austin." Then she whispered through her tears, "Like he pulled your daddy out nearly six years ago."

"What?" I was confused. Mr. Boudreaux's sudden connection with my daddy came out of nowhere for me. But only for a second. It was him on the bank watching me float down the creek. And the way he gripped my arm. Lafitte Boudreaux was a man possessed.

"Lafitte was gator baiting on Old Cypress Creek. Right about where you were grappling." She held on to my good arm. I helped her up. "Lafitte said he heard the engine, thought someone was speeding. He looked to the bridge in the distance in time to see your father flipping over the edge."

"He pulled Daddy out of the water?"

"Lafitte was on foot. Couldn't shortcut across in the creek because of the gators he had baited. By the time he ran up the hill to his house, got in his truck, and drove to the bridge . . . it was too late. Lafitte dove in anyway. The car was upside down and the windows were open."

Momma reached out, smoothing my hair and shaking her head.

"Unless it was pouring, your daddy always drove with the windows down. He played the outside of the car door like a drum, slapping his hand against it and tapping his fingers to the music." She stared down into the water. "Your daddy had a gash on his head, probably happened when the car flipped. He would've been unconscious when the car hit the water. When Lafitte finally got there, he pulled him out, dragged him to the bank. It was just too late."

Momma cried again, less hysterical this time and more sorrowful.

"I've never seen a man more broken than when Lafitte Boudreaux told me he didn't save your daddy."

"Momma, I didn't know he even knew Daddy." There was so much about my daddy that seemed locked away in a box somewhere. So much about who he was as a man, a friend. I wanted to know it all.

"Lafitte watched your father grow up, going in and out of Gray's True Value. Your daddy and his friends made a few late-night visits out to Possum Trot. Lafitte even taught him how to boil crawfish. He blamed himself for your daddy's death. Lafitte was gator baiting. It's illegal. He told me someday he'd make it right."

"But Daddy's wreck wasn't Mr. Boudreaux's fault," I argued.

"Choices have consequences, Austin." Momma moved closer to the Jeep. "The creek was probably full of gators. Had he been able to get in the water, he might have made it to your daddy in time. It's not his fault, and I've never blamed him. But I hope Lafitte feels he made it right to-night. Then he can put that demon to rest."

Water sloshed around my ankles. I watched Momma study the dark sky like she was looking for Orion's belt or some other heavenly evidence of order.

"Momma?" I couldn't leave Prosper Lake with anything unresolved. "You can't change Daddy's choice or his conse-quence. And you can't tie a lead rope around me like I'm some wayward FFA farm animal for the rest of my life."

Momma turned toward the bridge. She said nothing, just stared across the water as if she were watching Daddy's car slowly sink in the darkness.

"You taught me to pray the problem. You've always said only God knows for certain the outcome of our choices. Isn't that why you preached to me so much about praying the problem? So He can guide us towards better choices?"

She looked surprised that I remembered her Sunday school lecture. Or maybe Momma just realized that she'd spent the years since Daddy's death struggling to control outcomes and had lost the ability to let go and let God.

A car, careening down the hill, slowed as it neared the bridge. Momma's eyes followed the red taillights safely across.

"And I may shave the truth some, but I'm not reckless," I added.

Momma put her arm around my waist, squeezing me at her side. "I know, baby, I know."

elvis and daddy live on

The Texas heat melted July right into August. Summer afternoons in downtown Big Wells passed like funeral processions—quiet, slow, long. Customers at Gray's True Value came in before noon or not at all. It was just too blistering hot for folks to get out and walk the square. Momma thought it was the best time to clean. So Maribel and I, armed with cotton cloths and a spray bottle of vinegar water, dusted every piece of crystal and china in the store. Just how I wanted to spend my fifteenth birthday.

Maribel shined up a crystal cake stand, holding it up to the light coming through the window. "What kind of cake are you having for your birthday?" she asked.

"The kind the waitstaff at the Burger Barn brings out when they sing 'Happy Birthday' to you."

Maribel giggled.

My left arm was still a little sore, or I would've popped her with my cleaning cloth. She knew the Fourth of July firework details between me and Momma. She also knew

Momma didn't do parties. I was doomed to a life of strangers at restaurants clapping birthday shout-outs.

I thought I'd set Maribel straight.

"You know, Miss Quinceañera." I darn near rubbed the silver off a platter. "Need I remind you not everyone gets a big God-summoned church service and cultural festival on their birthday. You could be a little more sympathetic."

"Okay, Austin." Maribel pooched her bottom lip out. "I'm so sorry you're not Mexican."

I was just about to hit her with a few squirts of vinegar water when a window-rattling rumble filled downtown. The store vibrated like someone had bowled a cannonball down the wooden, center aisle. Maribel and I stopped dusting and ran to the window.

In the swirling heat rising from the pavement, Lewis Fortenberry, straddling an old purple metallic Harley-Davidson, rumbled to a stop in front of Gray's True Value.

"Holy cow!" I put the spray bottle down. Lewis's motorcycle had shotgun pipes and high chrome handlebars. "Elvis is a biker?"

Lewis took off his helmet, hung his sunglasses on the neck of his T-shirt, pulled a small comb from his back pocket, and groomed his hair into a ducktail style just like Elvis. Since the fair, Lewis had grown real sideburns, too—thick, black hockey sticks on his cheeks.

Maribel and I waved for him to come in. Lewis Forten-berry was like a rain shower in August—always glad to see it, always welcome.

Lewis turned the handle, then tapped his toe on the bot-tom of the door. It swung open like a slowly drawn curtain. Lewis didn't just enter the store. He made an entrance. He held a brown paper sack in one hand but stretched his arms wide. "Hey, hey, little mommas!" He shook his shoulders. "How about showin' Big Daddy some love?"

I side-hugged Lewis with my one good arm. Maribel kissed a hockey stick. She'd been all about the cheek-kissing since turning fifteen.

I looked Lewis over. He was definitely born in the wrong era. He had his white T-shirt tucked into his blue jeans, and his jelly-roll middle bounced with his every move. He looked like a busted can of biscuits. And he wore white, marching band shoes.

"Those don't really go with the motorcycle, Lewis." I pointed at his shoes.

"Chopper, baby, chopper. Vintage 1976. And these?" He jerked a knee to his chest, pointing his toe. "Well, little mom-mas, Elvis is moving from the back of the band to the front." He stuck his chest out like Charles Dickens and marched a high-step in place. "I'm going out for drum major, baby. The shoes and I are one."

Momma, in her boots, walked up with her hands on her hips like some Old West sheriff. "Hello there, Lewis."

Lewis faced her, working his best Elvis-in-a-gunfight. "Hello, Momma."

Momma tried not to smile when she saw him, but it was no use. Lewis Fortenberry brought out the joy in even the hardest of hearts.

"What can we do for you?" she asked.

"Blackberries," he said. Lewis stuck the sack out like he'd pulled a gun from a holster. "Straight off the vine. The folks said you asked for them."

I grabbed the sack before Momma could get it. Summer meant blackberries, and Lewis's family grew the best—big, juicy, the size of a grown man's thumb. I shoved my hand deep into the sack, plucked out a fat one, and popped it into my mouth.

"It's Austin's birthday." Momma handed me one of the cleaning cloths. I dabbed the reddish-blue juice from my chin.

"Happy birthday, baby," Lewis drawled. Then he dropped to one knee and kissed my hand. I thought he was about to sing.

"Birthday blackberries!" Maribel reached into the sack. "This could start a cultural tradition for you, Austin." She drew out a handful of plump berries.

I took my hand back from Lewis and showed Maribel my purple teeth. She'd really been acting full of herself.

Momma took the sack. "You know, Lewis . . ." She looked at the dwindling berries. "This is a pound. I could probably use another, maybe two more pounds."

Lewis stood up. "Well, Momma, I can make that happen for you. Just let me make another berry run."

"Can you bring them by the house?" Momma asked. "I'm closing early to take Austin to the Burger Barn for her birthday dinner."

Maribel and I locked eyes. "See?" I proved my point. Momma didn't do parties.

Maribel blinked and snickered like she knew something I didn't.

"We got you covered, Ms. Gray. Farm to market to home delivery." Lewis unhooked his sunglasses from his collar and flicked them open. "Little momma." Lewis put on his shades. Then he reached his hand out like he was bringing me out of an audience onto a stage. "You wanna ride?"

I was into my fourth or fifth blackberry, still dabbing juice. Lewis was serious.

"She doesn't have a helmet." Momma quickly jumped in.

Lewis held up two fingers like he was giving Momma the peace sign. "Always keep an extra on the back."

"You should go, Austin." Maribel walked over and stood by Momma as if she might have to prop her up. I loved that quality in Maribel. She was a doer. Maribel didn't talk about being friends; she just stepped up and acted like one.

I caught a glimpse of Lewis's bike outside. With my scrawny legs and arms and Lewis's chunky middle, we'd look like a cartoon: a praying mantis and a fat frog on a chopper. Dean Ottmer would certainly point that out, given the opportunity. But at the moment, I couldn't have cared less. I was drawn to that Harley like it was in my blood. I'd never ridden a motorcycle, and this might just be my one chance. "Just a short ride," I begged.

Momma rocked back and forth on the heels of her boots like she didn't know whether to move forward or stay back.

She finally rocked forward. "Oh, go ahead."

My mouth fell open. "You're serious?" I couldn't believe it. "You're going to let me ride a motorcycle with an Elvis impersonator?"

Lewis cringed like someone had twisted a knot in his ducktail. "Performance artist, baby, Elvis Performance Artist."

"Not exactly, Austin." Momma pointed outside. "I'm going to let you ride *that* motorcycle"—then she patted Lewis's back—"with *this* Elvis impersonator."

"Performance artist," Maribel corrected.

"Thank you. Thank you very much," Lewis said.

I hit the door running before Momma changed her mind.

The late afternoon sun had warmed Lewis's extra helmet. Momma pulled the chin strap tight.

"I'll be all right," I promised. "Remember, I'm not reckless."

Momma didn't say a single word. She grabbed my helmet and pulled me to her chest, holding my head in her hands, taking deep slow breaths.

Then she let me go.

Lewis switched on the chopper, revving the throttle back and forth — *bbbrrRRRRR-pow, pow, pow* — *bbbrrRRRRR-pow, pow, pow!*

I stood beside the roaring motorcycle, trying to figure out just how a girl in a miniskirt got on one of these things. It was higher than it looked.

Lewis tapped his right band shoe on a flat, chrome thingy. "Step on that!"

I steadied my foot, gripped Lewis's right shoulder, and threw my leg over the seat. I was on. Ready to ride. Really badass.

Then I read the sticker on the back of Lewis's helmet: WARNING: IN CASE OF RAPTURE, THIS VEHICLE WILL BE UNMANNED.

God's way of reminding me I wasn't riding with the Hell's Angels. No. I was rolling with Evangelical Elvis.

I put my arms around his doughnut waist. Lewis hit the throttle, thundering onto Main Street. We rounded the square once. I caught Lewis checking himself out in the reflection of the store windows. I caught him because I was doing the same thing. Clearance signs and end-of-summer sale banners plastered the windows. But I could watch myself riding by. I imagined Christmastime with the twinkling lights and the fat Santas and the parade. I practiced my sweetheart wave on Maribel and Momma as we passed Gray's True Value for the last time. Momma held on to a parking meter but tried to give her best thumbs-up.

Outside of downtown Big Wells, where the old pump jacks dot the farmland, Lewis glided onto Highway 37. Then he hit the throttle. Popped it hard. I slid back a little on the seat but held on to Lewis for dear life. Riding Lewis's Harley was a little like riding a fast bicycle with a deafening rumble. The heavy bike held the road, so I slowly let go of Lewis's jiggly middle. One hand at a time. The hot sun warmed the tops of my legs. I held out my arms. A little at first. Then full out. The rushing wind swept through me. No hands. This was freedom.

I remembered Momma's story about Daddy keeping his car windows rolled down. I closed my eyes and felt my father in the breeze.

Lewis slowed up, leaning the bike off the road to the fruit stand—a wooden platform the size of a barn, with corner posts holding up a rusty tin roof. A weathered old sign, probably as old as Gray's True Value and wide as a porch swing, leaned against an oak tree: FORTENBERRY FRUITS. A dozen or so cars lined the highway; a few zipped right up to the stand.

Lewis parked his Harley by a giant inflatable blackberry.

The ballooning purple berry seemed an odd contrast to the antique sign. I took off my helmet and asked him, "That's your idea, right?"

Lewis hung his helmet on a handlebar, took out his comb, and reshaped his ducktail. "That's right, little momma." Lewis checked his hair in the side mirror. "We've got a peach, a strawberry, and a blueberry, baby. Depends on the season." He held out his hand to help me off the bike. "In the fall, we've got a pecan."

"Only you would have a fifteen-foot inflatable nut!" I laughed.

"The king is one of a kind, baby."

I followed Lewis up the steps. The last time I could remember being at the fruit stand was with my daddy. My eyes wandered to the fields behind the platform; rows of berry vines and clusters of peach groves crawled over the rolling hills to the horizon.

Nothing had changed. I stood perfectly still, half expecting Daddy to sneak behind me and scoop me up.

Flatbed farm trucks backed up to the platform. Hispanic men in their wide-brimmed straw hats and bandanas unloaded crates of plump blackberries. Sweet, ripe cantaloupe perfumed the stand like a fragrant candle. Toddlers ran back and forth on the wood-planked platform, squealing to the pounding of their own feet. Men in suits just off from work stood in line between overalled farmers and tennis-skirted women. Lewis's family business served everyone. Just like Gray's True Value. Fortenberry Fruits felt like home.

"Austin Gray!" A frosty-haired lady with a twang like Paula Deen clamped me into a viselike hug. She was big as a Buick. Hugging her felt like falling face-first on a water bed. "Lewis Fortenberry, did you brang this child out here?"

"Yes, Aunt Lou." Lewis smiled at me. "Don't hurt her."

"Lord have mercy! Hurt this child! Let me tell you, your daddy—God rest his soul—used to brang you out here when you were no bigger than a watermelon."

I locked my knees and froze. No one ever brought up my daddy like that. Wide open and loud. I didn't know whether to smile or cry.

"I remember he'd nose around at these." Lewis's aunt Lou palmed a cantaloupe and shoved it under my nose. "You smell that? That's how you know it's ripe. The more it smells a strong sweet, the riper it is. Breathe, child!"

I took a big whiff. It was like being filled to the toes with citrus and honeysuckle.

"Your daddy would go through a dozen before he sniffed out one that was perfect." She threw her head back and cackled. "He used to say that's how he found your momma, too!"

I held on to the cantaloupe and smiled. I could've listened to her for days.

Lewis filled a green mesh container with berries, then placed them onto an old scale hanging from the stand's rafters. "Two pounds," he said.

He dropped the berries into a brown paper bag. "Ready to ride?"

"Add this." I pitched him the cantaloupe.

"Now, darlin'." Aunt Lou put her arm around me. "Don't you be such a stranger. You come out anytime. I've got the goods on your daddy, and I'm gonna tell off on him."

"Yes, ma'am." I looked around the fruit stand. "I'll be back."

The evening sun, low on the horizon, flamed the sky in purples and fire reds. Somehow, between the Harley ride and cantaloupe, I felt closer to my dad. He was a life worth talking about.

This was the best birthday ever.

Lewis and I rolled back onto the highway, back into town, turning onto Camellia Heights. My street was quiet, almost too quiet. Too hot for joggers. Too late for children. Dean and Sammy Ottmer would be at the evening practice for football two-a-days.

Lewis cruised to a stop in front of my house. A beat-up flatbed truck was backed into the driveway. Just as I took off my helmet, I spotted Lafitte Boudreaux slipping around the side, carrying a small shovel.

There were only two things that could possibly connect Lafitte Boudreaux, my backyard, and a short shovel: Charles Dickens and death.

a birthday boil

Charles Dickens was fat. No way of getting around it. Since the fair, I hadn't watched him too closely. Customers at the store fed him constantly. And if they didn't, he'd perch by the front door and pop his wings out when they'd try to leave. He darn near demanded everyone feed him. But in chickens, fat builds first around the heart. Charles Dickens's heart could've been stressed. Seeing Lafitte Boudreaux with a shovel, I feared Charles Dickens might have met his maker. And sometimes, when a girl grows up under a cloud of tragedy, she starts to expect it.

My best birthday quickly soured.

I jumped off Lewis's Harley and headed along the side of my house toward the back gate. If something had happened to Charles Dickens, it would be all my fault. He was my responsibility, and he deserved better.

"Austin, wait!" Lewis huffed and puffed behind me.

I stopped at the gate.

Lewis was bent over with his hands on his knees, sweating like Elvis at the end of a performance. "Your fruit," he wheezed.

"Something's happened to my rooster, Lewis." I unlatched the gate, ignoring the brown sack on the ground. "I just know it."

When the sun drifts below the horizon, the evening darkens to a hazy purple. The clicking tree frogs and whirring locusts tune their night symphony. The lightning bugs start their glowing.

Twilight comes down.

I pushed open the gate.

The backyard was lit up like some kind of festival. Tiki torches burned and Christmas lights hung in swags from the trees. Newspapers covered the picnic table. Maribel popped open a bag of tortilla chips and put them out next to what looked like a bowl of her mamanita's *pico de gallo*. And Sundi Knutt, sipping on a bottle of root beer, stretched out on the glider in some shorty-shorts with her bare feet in Ricky's lap. Maribel spotted me.

"Austin's here!" she yelled.

Momma rushed out from the kitchen. She carried a big tray loaded with potatoes in mesh sacks, corn on the cob, and sausage. She sat the tray down on a patio table. Beside her, Daddy's old outdoor Cajun cooker steamed over a hot flame. Behind the rising gray mist, with his face hidden under his dusty hat, Lafitte Boudreaux stirred the pot with that shovel.

"Happy birthday, Austin." Momma threw her hands open like some awkward clown. "Surprise!"

169

So much for birthday dreams. This was a nightmare. I couldn't take my eyes off that boiling pot.

"Where's Charles Dickens?" I asked.

Sundi hopped through the grass on her tiptoes. She squeezed me. "Surprise, surprise, surprise!"

"Where's Charles Dickens?" I was on the verge of tears. For a moment, I thought they had done the unthinkable. These people had all gone nuts. Maybe I was just having some guilt-ridden anxiety dream. "Pinch me, Lewis. Tell me this isn't happening."

"Oh, it's happening, baby," Lewis said. Sundi had moved from greeting me to Lewis. She was all hugged up on him. "It is *sooo* happening."

"Momma, where's Charles Dickens?" I headed for the boiling pot.

Momma grabbed my shoulders. "Austin, look!"

Charles Dickens waddled across the patio like a fat penguin. He spotted Maribel with a chip and popped his wings out.

I fell into a chair.

"Austin," Maribel said. "You're as white as coconut milk."

The backyard seemed to spin around in the Christmas lights.

"Happy birthday." Josh Whatley cowboyed up in front of me. He touched the toes of his boots to mine. "You surprised?"

My feet melted. "You could say that." I collected myself and wished more than anything for a hairbrush.

Sundi, Ricky, and Lewis walked up. Momma and Maribel crowded around my chair.

"This is really, really something," I said, "and I am surprised. More than anyone will ever know." It took a minute for me to take in everybody. Momma, Maribel, Josh, Ricky, Sundi, and Lewis. I drew a bead on Lewis, making sure he understood to keep a tight lip on my rooster assumption. They were all here. A party on my birthday. "Thanks, Momma."

"Don't thank me, Austin." Momma shook her head. "This is all Maribel."

"It's not exactly a *quinceañera*." Maribel kissed my cheek. "But happy birthday."

Lafitte Boudreaux snuck up behind Momma and tapped her shoulder. She headed to the cooker. Josh was still in front of me. Boot to boot.

I followed the long line of denim from Josh's boots to his waist. He wore a plaid short-sleeved shirt with the sleeves rolled up tight around his biceps. His tan biceps. When I stood up, he didn't back up. My nose raked the center button on his shirt. He smelled like candy. *Black licorice,* I thought. Sweet and spicy; love it or leave it alone.

Josh put his finger under my chin. Made me look in his green eyes. "I need to go help your momma." Then he turned around.

"You know he's a cutie." Maribel pointed a chip at Josh as he walked off. "With a bootie."

Since her *quinceañera*, Maribel had opened up like a spring gardenia.

"How'd you do all this?" I asked her.

"Your momma really did help. She even called Sundi and Josh, so they'd know they were welcome and that she wasn't still mad from the Fourth of July. And she got Lafitte Boudreaux here."

"What is he doing here?" I looked over at the cooker. Josh was standing by him, pouring salt into a big, round galvanized bucket.

"Austin, come watch." Sundi, along with everyone else, was hovering near the cooker.

I walked up, wholly embarrassed that I ever thought they'd cook my rooster.

Momma pointed at the bucket. "Take a look."

And I did. Crawling all around in the bucket full of salted water were small lobster-looking things. Mudbugs. Crawdads.

Momma smiled. "Maribel wanted you to have your own cultural celebration. So we're having a crawfish boil. It's as close as I could get, and no doubt it's what your father would've done. Lafitte's here to make sure we Texans do it right."

"Miss Aus'in, ya best step out tha way."

Lafitte Boudreaux covered the bucket with a piece of chicken wire fashioned into a lid. "Ya boys"—he pointed at Josh and Ricky—"get on da rinse. Ah'd say they's purged."

"You mean they . . . ?" I covered my mouth.

"Let's just say the salt water cleans them out." Josh winked at me. Then he and Ricky each grabbed a handle and turned the bucket upside down, pouring out the polluted water.

Lewis put his arm around my momma. "Did I mention I'm a vegetarian, baby?"

"Did I mention that your aunt Lou neglected to tell me you'd be picking up Austin on a motorcycle?" Momma dropped the corn and sausages into the cooker full of boiling water.

"He knew?" I was starting to believe this party took some elaborate planning.

Sundi took my hand. "I have to show you something else." The light was on in the kitchen, and we looked through the patio window. A layered chocolate cake in the shape of a boot sat on the counter. "Maribel," Sundi said.

I watched Maribel as she nosed around Lafitte Boudreaux. She had her own interests that were different from mine, and she seemed to lead another life literally on the other side of the tracks. She might have other friends; I might have other friends. But Maribel had the best friend spot sewn up.

Josh and Ricky watered down and rinsed the crawfish two more times. Then they toted the bucket next to the cooker.

"Step back now," Lafitte Boudreaux ordered.

Josh hoisted the bucket up. The muscles in his arms flexed. He looked like Atlas holding up the world. Josh dumped the crawling crawfish into the boiling water. Lafitte Boudreaux shut off the flame, stuck in the shovel, and stirred.

" 'Bout ten, fifteen minutes."

"What all can we put in there?" Maribel quizzed Lafitte Boudreaux. In her mind, she was probably trying to figure out some Mexican-Texan-Cajun concoction.

"Anything ya wahns." Mr. Boudreaux kept stirring.

Maribel ran into the house and came charging back out with a handful of green leafy things. Cilantro. She tore the herb into pieces and dropped it into the pot.

Momma motioned for everyone to find a seat at the picnic table. "No plates. No utensils. No napkins."

Lafitte Boudreaux held a basket full of boiled crawfish with the potatoes and sausage and corn mixed in. Then he pitched them all out onto the newspapered table. Cooked, the crawfish turned bright red with curled-up tails.

I didn't remember much about my daddy's crawfish boils. "I have no idea how to eat these things." I held one between my thumb and index finger. It looked like something you'd find in a souvenir shop at the beach. I wasn't even sure I wanted to eat one.

Sundi was into her third crawfish. "Look, Austin." She dismembered a fourth. "Just twist the tail off and get the meat out." Then she put her shiny-glossed lips around the thorax and sucked out the juice. Impressive.

I was close to feeling overshadowed at my own birthday party by a crawfish-head-sucking marshmallow girl when Josh Whatley reached around me from behind.

"Pinch here," he said, grabbing the lower end of the bug. "Then twist the tail off."

I did that. I think. I was a little dizzy with his arms around me.

"Now." Josh peeled the crunchy tail away from the meat with his thumbs. "Think shrimp."

I took the little piece of meat out and ate it. Spicy, a little randy-tasting.

Josh handed me the rest of the crawfish, the hull with the head still on it. "You can suc—" He turned red.

I turned what I'm certain was a lovely shade of ruby. "I know, I know." I snatched the thing from him, thinking I'd die if the words *suck the head* came out of Josh Whatley's mouth. Furthermore, I'd stick with the tail meat. I dropped the hull in a cardboard box at the end of the table.

Lafitte Boudreaux had disappeared into the night. Momma cleaned around the cooker. She walked around, carrying a trash bag. Still always moving, but this time the corners of her mouth turned up, not down. She was smiling.

Sitting on the bench around the picnic table between Maribel and Josh, I listened to Sundi giggle, watched Lewis put on a hip-swinging show, laughed at Ricky refilling Sundi's drink and condiment orders. I thought about

Maribel's *quinceañera*. There were lots of things I didn't have, like a last doll or a crown or a pair of high heels. But I had Christmas lights in August and mudbugs and friends and a new connection with my daddy. I knew my past, and that gave me a new strength.

Little did I know I was going to need every last bit of it.

some things never change

Even Maribel noticed a change in Momma.

We spent Saturday afternoon painting the storefront windows for the Big Wells spirit-filled fall. Football season. I was three weeks into my sophomore year. My arm was almost all healed except for a stripe of scaly, pink skin and a few itchy, brown scabs. Momma had a shine about her.

"Your momma's like seven-minute icing," Maribel said. "She rolls on at a hard boil, but when she's done, she's velvety smooth and easy to work with."

Momma stepped onto the sidewalk in front of Gray's True Value wearing Daddy's old football jersey, number 68. She still wore her boots and jeans, but the black shirts were gone. I hadn't seen her in a black shirt since July.

"How close are you two to finishing?" She held Charles Dickens in her arms like a baby.

"We just have to draw the roughneck."

"HAAAWK!" Charles Dickens stretched his neck out and crowed at the sight of Mayor Nesmith charging up the sidewalk.

"Jeannie! Jeannie!" He hollered to keep her from ducking into the store.

Momma didn't move. She just shut her eyes and rubbed on Charles Dickens's wattle. She was back to praying the problem.

"Nice job, ladies." Nesmith checked out our team-spirit paint job. "But you misspelled *defense*."

Maribel and I stepped back from the window.

"D-E-F-E-N-S-E," Maribel spelled aloud.

"Hah!" Nesmith laughed. His beer belly shook. "D-E-F-E-N-*C*-E."

I wanted to whack him with my paint-dipped brush. But I caught sight of the nubs in the middle of his hairy left hand. The Fourth of July left a mark on him, too.

The story around town was that Mayor Nesmith and a bunch of his cronies partied on his barge in the middle of Prosper Lake until long after the fireworks were over. Woozy from alcohol and propped up with false confidence, Mayor Nesmith attempted to split a watermelon with his new butcher knife in one slice. He miscalculated or a wave hit the barge. Regardless, Nesmith failed to pull back his left hand, the one holding the melon steady. He severed the three middle fingers with that butcher knife. Nearly died from the loss of blood. That's the part the mayor talks about.

"Jeannie." He put his full-fingered hand, the right one, over his heart, tilted his head back, and spoke as if he were searching for God's face in the sky. "Since my life-changing accident, the wife and I have joined Full Grace Faith

Community Church." He glanced down for a moment to make sure Momma was still with him. "I can't tell you what a blessing it has been, and what a new calling I have as mayor of Big Wells."

"New group of voters," I whispered to Maribel.

I didn't trust his born-again behavior. As far as I was concerned, true change only comes from brokenness, and I hadn't seen Nesmith in the Prosper Lake mud at the bitter end of heartbreak.

"I nearly bled to death." Nesmith all but doubled over. "Christ shed his blood for us, and I feel I shed my blood for greater good in this blessed community." Nesmith stuck his good hand out and tried to pet Charles Dickens. The rooster's hackles stiffened straight up.

"What exactly do you want, Victor?" Momma saw right through him. "Exactly."

"Church needs a coffeepot." Nesmith emerged from his born-again shroud. "A big one. Twenty, thirty cup." He glanced at the numbers on Momma's jersey. "Cup size very important," he stumbled. "Care to donate?"

"I'll give the church a coffeepot." Momma seemed tickled. "A big-cup one," she laughed, opening the door to the store. "Victor, I'll gladly give the church a coffeepot as long as you'll agree to stay in attendance. It might just do you some good."

"Did she seem silly to you?" I asked Maribel as Momma went in the store.

"Not silly, just happy." We watched Momma through

the window. She handed Nesmith a large box, walked him back to the door, and all but shoved him out—grinning the whole time.

"He doesn't seem to bother her like he used to," I said.

Momma reminded me of the parade sweethearts, just smiling and moving on despite the jerk in their presence. She seemed like a load had been lifted ever since she opened up about Daddy's death and his being gone. A fresh trust in the divine order of things.

Nesmith tucked the box under his right arm as he passed by.

"Hang loose, girls!" He raised his lame left hand and gave us the Hawaiian sign—the one a normal hand makes by holding down the three middle fingers and extending the thumb and pinky. It was the only wave Nesmith could do with that hand. "Hang loose, baby!"

Maribel and I snickered, then went back to our painting.

"He has to know we think he's an idiot," I said, drawing the roughneck's scowl.

"Mamanita has a saying. *Árbol que crece torcido, jamás su tronco endereza*." Maribel dipped her brush in the paint. "A tree which grows bent will never get straight."

Tires squealed around the corner. A truck skidded to a rubber-burning stop in front of Gray's True Value: OTTMER FORD COURTESY VEHICLE, according to the sign on the driver's-side door. Dean Ottmer sat behind the wheel.

"Why isn't he at football practice?" I wondered aloud.

A white-haired old man staggered from the truck. He steadied himself with one hand on the truck's side; the other patted his forehead with a handkerchief. Maribel and I dropped our paintbrushes and rushed to help him to the sidewalk.

"Dude!" Dean rolled down the window and hollered. "I don't have to sit here and wait, do I?"

The old man ran the handkerchief around his neck. "I'll just be a minute."

Dean left his window down and turned up the radio.

"I took my car in for an oil change," the old man explained as we guided him into the store. "They said, '*Take the courtesy truck. Take the courtesy truck if you need to run an errand.*'"

He rubbed his right shoulder.

"He slung me against that door at every turn. Slammed on the brakes at every stop. And that pounding, yap-yap music!"

"I bet Ms. Gray will drive you back." Maribel nodded at me.

"Yeah," I added. "I'll tell the driver you're not riding with him again."

The old man thanked Maribel over and over as she walked him up the center aisle.

I went to break the news to Dean. I stood on the sidewalk with my hands on my hips and yelled over Dean's bass. "He's not coming back!"

Dean ignored me.

"He's not coming back! You can leave!"

Dean turned the truck off and got out. "He has to come back. I'm his ride, special ed." He smiled big when he called me that. *Special ed* and *retard* were two of his favorite pet names for me.

"He won't get back in the truck with you, Dean. He said your driving stinks." I grinned. That last part might have been a summary, but it was the truth. I tapped the heel of my boot against the sidewalk, folded my arms, and watched Dean's rage split him in two like a chopped log of firewood.

Dean tore into the store—flinging the door back and stomping down the hardwood, leaving the frail crystal ting-tinging in his wake. By sheer force of personality, he tried to snuff out any notions the old man had of not getting back in the truck. Dean flat-out demanded the old man ride with him back to the dealership.

"You're violating company policy!" Dean shifted his weight. Had the man been younger, I think Dean Ottmer would've punched him. "I have to drive you back to the dealership."

"Not happening, Dean." Momma eased him away from the old man. "You tell your father if he has any problems with my driving the gentleman back, he'll need to come pick him up himself."

I opened the door as she ushered Dean out.

He pulled a cell phone out of his pocket and paced on

the sidewalk. I followed Dean outside and pretended to finish painting.

"That's not fair! I don't want to wash cars!" Dean screamed into the phone, then turned on me.

"This is all your fault, pencil legs!"

I did my best to ignore him and keep painting, but I saw my knobby knees reflected in the window. I had to stand up to him.

"You were driving like a maniac, Dean. I had nothing to do with that."

"You talked him into not getting back in the truck with me. You know you did."

Dean stood with his arms folded and his legs apart. His athletic shorts covered his calves and the crotch hung down to his knees.

"You're only fifteen. How'd you get a license anyway?" I kept a paintbrush in my hand in case I needed to defend myself.

"I got it so I could work, retard. It's a hardship license."

"They give you a booster seat with that?" It just came out like a sudden hiccup. I dropped my paintbrush and froze. Dean hated, more than anything, for someone to point out what a short stump he was.

"You are so going down!" he threatened and jerked open the truck door. "You're gonna wish your daddy was around, 'cause I'm your worst nightmare." He cranked the truck and raced the engine.

"Tell me something I don't know, Dean." I acted like he didn't scare me, like his slam about my daddy didn't hurt.

"You'll find out." He smoked the truck's tires, keeping one foot on the brake and the other pressed on the accelerator. Then he peeled out.

Maribel swung open the door. "Are you okay?"

"I'm fine," I lied. "He's got roid rage and he spouted a bunch of empty threats."

"Like what?"

"Said he's my worst nightmare and I'll find out." I picked up the paints and brushes. "He's probably headed to wrap my house."

But he didn't wrap our house. Not Saturday night and not Sunday night. I even got up before dawn on Sunday to check. No toilet paper anywhere.

I left for school on Monday no more than a twinge uneasy. I had AP classes again and FFA when Dean had football. We didn't have the same lunch. I rarely crossed his path.

Lewis Fortenberry sat by me in first-period English.

"Hey, baby," he greeted me every morning in his Elvis voice.

"I heard the football team is picked to win District." I chatted with him before the bell rang to start class. "Guess that means the band will have a long marching season."

"Maybe so, maybe not." He fell into Elvis again. "You see, darlin', the football team lost one of their fullbacks."

"He got hurt?"

"Hurt himself," Lewis said. "Dean Ottmer failed the ol' pee test. Looks like he spent the summer popping muscle candy."

"It took a pee test for them to figure that out?" I remembered his angry outbursts. "Think they'll suspend him?"

"For a few days, maybe."

And the school did. Dean Ottmer was out of school three whole days.

By Thursday of that week, rain had moved in. I always walked with Sundi and Josh to the agriculture classroom, a metal building behind the school. Josh carried me in piggyback, so my boots wouldn't get wet and muddy. He backed up to a table, lowering me onto it. Sundi put Ricky on her back and backed him up to the table. I laughed. Sundi laughed. Everyone laughed. Being in FFA was like family.

"Austin Gray!"

I scooted from behind Josh and down the table to see who called my name. Dean Ottmer smirked at me and handed a schedule-change form to the teacher. Kicked out of football, Dean had signed up for FFA.

boo! guess who!

Dean Ottmer had an answer for everything.

The ag teacher, an older man with a gray handlebar mustache, announced one day: "We'll need parent drivers for the trip to the Houston Livestock Show and Rodeo."

"Dude, that's stupid," Dean said.

The ag teacher twisted one of the curled ends of his mustache.

"Nobody wants to go on a school trip with a bunch of parents. I'll get some vans from the dealership." Dean leaned back in his chair with his legs spread wide and clasped his hands behind his head. "Tricked out with video. My kind of movies, if you know what I mean." He showed his teeth and stuck his fist out for one of the boys to tap.

No one tapped. No one moved. No one wanted to ride with him. They left Dean with his fist hanging in midair.

On another day, when the teacher announced the grapefruit and orange fund-raising sale, Dean remarked, "That's stupid. I'm not selling fruit. I'll tell my dad to sponsor."

"This is agriculture economics, Dean." Josh made an

attempt to reason with him. "We study agriculture products and sell agriculture products to learn about the business of agriculture."

A light seemed to flash in Dean's eyes, a mini eureka. "That's stupid when you can get Farm Aid."

Ricky pretended to bang his head on the table.

Once, the teacher asked me to bring samples of different kinds of wire sold at Gray's True Value. "I want us to examine the wire's shape and durability to determine its appropriate use in caging and fencing various animals," he said.

Dean blurted, "Good, we can put Austin back in her pen." Dean howled alone. He raised both hands for a friend-clap to punctuate his joke. No takers. They isolated his hands in the air.

Josh shifted.

The ag teacher, a man who looked uncomfortable behind a desk but probably spent his weekends castrating cattle, took out a pocketknife and started cleaning out from under his fingernails. "Mr. Ottmer, everyone has had enough of your mouth."

"Dude, that's illegal." Dean pointed at the knife and looked around at all of us. He seemed to be the only one concerned. "That's a weapon, dude. They're gonna bust you. You can't have that on campus."

Josh scooted his chair back.

The air conditioner kicked on, and I noticed for the first time that there were no windows in the ag building.

Josh walked up behind Dean and leaned over him.

My heart raced, but I didn't budge. No one said a word. It was eerie, like being in a dark cave with nothing but the *shhhh-shhhh* warning from a rattlesnake.

I thought I heard Josh whisper, "What happens in the ag building stays in the ag building."

Dean's eyes darted around the room. No backup. He shoved a spiral notebook, sent it spinning onto the floor. "Man, you hicks are screwed up," Dean mumbled.

Unfortunately, after a few weeks and given Dean's compromised memory capacity, he seemed to forget Josh's warning. Slowly but surely, Dean picked back up where he'd left off. He dogged me every chance he got, so I kept a low profile. My life was easier without Dean being a factor. I never commented on his smack. I even stayed outside of the building until right about time for class to start. When I went in, I ducked behind Sundi and sat by Josh at the end of a long table. Actually, I sat behind him. I hid behind his broad shoulders. I avoided Dean's stork jokes by having Sundi turn in my papers for me. Dean dodging went on for the rest of September and October.

"How long do you think you can keep avoiding him?" Sundi asked one day while I waited for the bell to ring to go into class.

"Until after the holidays, maybe." Although I never argued with her when she brought it up, I had never told Sundi about wanting to be a sweetheart in the parade. I didn't want her to think I was using her or anyone else in the FFA. They were real friends, genuine.

"Austin," Josh said. "Just go in. Be yourself. Nobody listens to what Dean Ottmer says anyway."

The FFA had been different from other kids in other classes. Dean's slams weren't even acknowledged, not even laughed at. They treated Dean like one of those gag-gift, talking bass fish — not wanted and not really all that funny. But I was the one he targeted. Whether they believed his smack or not, laughed or not, it didn't matter. Dean Ottmer's insults embarrassed me in front of the entire FFA, embarrassed me to the core. I didn't care to live that, day in day out.

"I'm staying off his radar," I repeated for the umpteenth time.

If I could just make it to the parade, be the FFA Sweetheart, then I'd have something to trump his insults. He could slam my legs, my butt, my brains, my boobs. It wouldn't matter. I'd have sweetheart to throw down. I'd have a title to take on the high road.

"He shuts up if you punch him." Sundi was serious.

"I'm not like you." Sundi was the marshmallow girl, puffed with confidence. She had been sweetheart.

Josh and Sundi supported me, though. They hung outside before class and shielded me going in. With their help, I managed to avoid any major incidents with Dean during the fall semester. That is, until Halloween.

October thirty-first *would* have to fall on a weekday.

Maribel and I stood on the sidewalk in front of Big Wells High. A posse of popular kids strutted by in khaki

189

uniforms with names like *Juan* and *Jose* Sharpied on the shirt pockets. One even carried a leaf blower.

"I bet they'll get sent home for that," I said.

Maribel rolled her eyes. We both knew that even if a teacher wrote them up for discipline, the most the prin- cipal would do would be to keep the leaf blower in the office.

Two girls, with their lips outlined in brown, gloated past in maternity blouses and fake baby bumps. *"Hola!"* They waved at Maribel. Then they fell into each other, snorting at their own joke.

I wanted more than anything to crawl under a rock. "What are they thinking?"

Maribel watched them laugh their way into the main building. "It's Halloween, Austin. They're dressed as what scares them the most." Maribel's black eyes lit up. She reached into her Frida Kahlo purse and pulled out a bag of candy corn, the mixed kind with the little pumpkins in it. "Happy Halloween, Austin." She pitched the bag to me. "Share some with Lewis first period. I'm off to culinary arts." Maribel all but skipped away from the main entrance to the vocation outbuildings.

I wished I knew her secret for spinning hate-filled slurs to my own advantage.

Lewis Fortenberry met me in front of the school. His hair was slicked back, and he was in head-to-toe black with a wide, gold belt.

"I thought you might let *Elvis baby* walk you to first

190

period." Lewis started along the sides of the school—not through the main entrance.

"Wrong way, Elvis." I moved toward the front double doors.

A girl in an enormous, feather-trimmed witch hat cut ahead of me.

"Let's go around back, Austin." Lewis used his real voice, almost pleading.

"Don't be shy. If I had your confidence, I'd dress in costume, too." I pulled open the doors. "You look cool."

A crowd of onlookers hunkered together in the school's main foyer. Dean Ottmer positioned himself in the middle, at the bottom of the stairs, under the fluorescent light. I walked smack-dab into the middle of Dean's stunt and froze.

Dean Ottmer stood in front of me in a denim miniskirt, cowboy boots, and a brown wig. A featherless rubber chicken with a blue first-place ribbon pinned to it drooped in Dean's hand. No one could mistake the fact that I was his Halloween costume. But that wasn't the worst part. Upon my entrance, he shed his jacket and showed off a tank top with a piece of cardboard pinned underneath. It made his chest flat as the side of a box.

"Boo!" He waved both hands at me. "Guess who!" A rumble of laughter rolled over me like a bowling ball hitting a pin.

Dean attempted a supermodel runway prance—stopping in front of me, taking a slow catwalk turn. He flashed his no-profile chest, working the crowd.

"Dean-O! Dean-O! Dean-O!" a den of boys chanted and whistled.

A fall's worth of Dean-dodging down the drain. He must've known all the time that he was taking my humiliation schoolwide.

I didn't want Dean to see me cry, to let him know he got me. I didn't even have a second to pray the problem. I took off. Bumping into boys dressed as cheerleaders and girls in robes with cold cream on their faces, I ran to first period. Dean followed for a short distance, long enough to get the crowd charged up with his mock-sissy run.

I fell into my desk in English class and cried onto the desktop. The picture of Dean's flat cardboard chest and ridiculous denim miniskirt and boots flashed over and over in my head. *Oh, my God! I couldn't be more of a laughingstock.*

"I'm sorry, Austin." Lewis sat down by me. "I heard in the band hall he was up to something, a Halloween prank. I should've stopped you from going in."

"Not your fault," I sniffled and reached for my backpack. "I'm going to the nurse, going home."

The warning bell rang.

"Sit tight," Lewis said. "He expects you to run home. That's how he keeps his so-called friends. The more people start standing up to him, the more people will stand up to him."

"I'm outta here, Lewis." I felt like someone struck a match on my neck. My faced burned red. I wanted to change — out of my boots, out of my miniskirt, out of my life.

"Every time he slams you or anybody else, he's showing his cronies what can happen if they don't fall in line. You're different, Austin. You can stand up to him."

"I'm different, all right." I mocked him. "That's the problem."

Lewis sat quietly for a minute. I swear I thought he was praying for divine guidance.

"Austin." He dried his sweaty forehead with the bell sleeve of his costume. "Elvis said once that the truth is like the sun. You can shut it out, but it ain't going away. What happens if you don't run, you let it go? If you're just you? Boots, miniskirt, and all?"

"I don't always run. I've avoided him. I've ignored him." I buried my face in my backpack and mumbled, "He always comes back to me." I cried the words I'd thought since fourth grade. "If I had a father, I don't think he'd pick on me so much." I thought about Mr. Malvo Whiskers and his precious, protected nest. "I live in an unprotected nest."

"A nest?" Lewis rubbed his head with his gaudy, ring-covered hand. "You do have a father, Austin. A heavenly father who loves and protects you. And your earthly father is with him."

I picked my head up. As if my day couldn't get any worse, I was about to be preached to by an Evangelical Elvis impersonator.

"Lewis, I'm a joke. Everything about me. Please don't start on me being a sinner to boot."

Lewis took my backpack off my desk and put it on the

floor. "All I'm saying is, you're never alone, and God made everyone unique with different gifts. Now, that's not to say it doesn't sting a little when someone points yours out."

Lewis tugged at the gold sequin belt stretched around his waist. "It hurts, but you can't let it define you. Otherwise you'll wind up a hypocrite like Mayor Nesmith. And personally, I'd let God deal with Dean."

The final bell rang, signaling the start of first period.

Lewis stuck out his arm. Once again, I wiped my tears on Elvis's satin sleeve.

"You're not going to start singing 'Amazing Grace,' are you?"

Lewis and I chuckled as I dabbed my cheeks with his sleeve.

"*Don't be cruel,*" Elvis crooned.

I stayed at school and wore myself out for two class periods coming to terms with Dean Ottmer. It wasn't the Prosper Lake mud; I found my broken place inside the cinder-block walls of Big Wells High. I prayed the problem one last time. *Lord, Dean Ottmer is present. I can't avoid him. I can't reason with him.* Then it hit me. I gave up control. I let go and let God.

I can't change him, so please change me.

I settled down, a strange peace. Elvis was right. I wiggled my toes in my boots. They were a gift from my momma, and I loved them. My legs were pencils, but shapely. "Pickles will make you have pretty legs," I remember Daddy saying. He'd always buy me a huge pickle at football games. I was built like him, lean. When I looked in the mirror, when I looked at my legs, I saw my daddy. I just might wear skirts forever. Then there's Charles Dickens. Somehow, I managed to wind up with a Bantam rooster for a pet and a scar from grappling. That's just me, just how I roll.

Dean wasn't dramatizing to the school anything they didn't already know. Austin Gray: the boots, the daddy, the rooster, and the whole zany package. Maybe that was Maribel's secret. She never tried to shut out the sun.

I left second period, all but running to the ag building.

Josh and Sundi—heck, most of the FFA—waited for me outside. Several boys were decked out in full-blown cowboy gear. Halloween gave them a chance to wear their hats. Sundi had on a baby-pink lacy dress. She was Little Bo Peep. They all looked long-faced and grim.

"Who died?" I scooted front and center in my boots.

Josh pulled me into his arms and under his hat. "None of us are going in."

I wiggled out of his hug. "What? Why?"

"Dean's in there," Sundi said softly, her blue eyes tear-filled, but she sounded ticked. "He won't leave, so we did."

Josh tried hugging me again. It was his way of making things better. He wasn't the butt kicker that Little Bo Peep was.

"No, thank you." I garbled my words. "I mean thanks but no, no way."

"Let us do this for you, Austin." Sundi really felt sorry for me. They all did. But this time sympathy didn't sting.

"I'm good, really." I tried convincing them. "Think about it. Dean Ottmer is in the ag building in a wig and a skirt." Ricky and a couple other boys laughed out loud. "I wouldn't miss this for anything."

Josh and Sundi raised their eyebrows at each other. They had every reason to think I'd come unhinged.

"I'm really, really okay. I'm not the joke. I get that now." I grabbed both their hands and walked into the ag building.

Dean Ottmer, still in his Austin Gray costume, sat on a table with one leg stretched out and his back to us. He was posed like the girl outlines on the mud flaps of an eighteen-wheeler.

I snuck up behind him. "Boo!" I snickered. "Guess who!"

decision time

fter Halloween, Dean's smack seemed to roll off me like water off a duck's back, but I still wanted to be a parade sweetheart. I had spent too much time and gone to too much trouble for that not to happen. But my becoming a hood ornament in the No-Jesus Christmas Parade hinged on one circumstance: The FFA chapter elected their sweetheart. A simple matter of votes. Other than Sundi, I was the only girl with a blue-ribbon farm animal. I didn't have a deer hunting license, but the pink scar on my left arm gave me sportsman creds. Sundi had already been sweetheart. Not even Dean Ottmer could screw up my odds.

I was back to sitting on the table in the building before class.

"Here, retard." Dean came in one day close to Thanksgiving and threw down a used Christmas gift bag. "Merry Christmas, stork."

I didn't put my hand in the bag. I turned it upside down and shook it. My skullcap, the purple-and-black check, the one Dean stuck down the front of his pants, fell out. Dean choked up a "Hoorah!" and shadowboxed around in a little Dean dance.

"Any-*way*." I drew the *way* part out and returned to my conversation with Josh and Sundi. Ricky got a ruler from the teacher's desk. He gently lifted the cap, balancing it on the end of the ruler, and dropped it in the trash. Like everything Dean Ottmer did or said, whatever he tried to accomplish with the "gift" was simply irrelevant to all but him.

He kicked a chair away from a table with a hard swipe of his foot. He dropped onto the chair, put his legs up on the table, and clasped his hands behind his head. "Sundi," he growled.

"What is it, Dean?" Sundi had her hands on her hips. Her blue eyes seemed to darken.

Dean had given up trying to bully the boys into being his friends, so he worked on Sundi. He was over the fact that she had slugged him. I actually think he may have liked it or maybe he wanted to get her back somehow. Either way, he knew her weakness. Dean figured out that if the marshmallow girl felt sorry for him, she'd pay him some attention.

"Come here," he ordered. Dean sat away from everyone else. "C'mon, nobody talks to me. I got something to show you."

Sundi sucked in a big breath, like she was going under for a catfish. She stomped toward him, stopping just out of his arm's reach. "What?"

Dean pointed at his feet. He had new boots. "Lucchese, eight hundred dollars."

"That's nice." She turned her back on him.

The ag teacher came into the room. I slid off the table and into a chair. Sundi plopped down beside me.

"We need to elect a female representative for this chapter of the Future Farmers of America to participate in the upcoming Christmas parade," he said. His handlebar mustache twittered. "I'll take nominations, then we'll vote."

The representative would be the sweetheart. I fidgeted with the zipper on my backpack. Zip-zip, zip-zip, up and down. This was it. The whole year had come down to this moment.

Sundi put her hand over my nervous zipping. "I would like to nominate Austin." Then she looked at me and smiled her sugary sweet, marshmallow-girl smile. I piggybacked her confidence and sat up straight.

"Oh, God!" Dean Ottmer flung his arms and his legs, spreading them wide. He looked like he'd been speared in the chest and impaled onto the chair. "You've got to be kidding."

"Ottmer, if you have something to say, it better be constructive," the teacher warned.

"Shouldn't we have a sweetheart that at least looks like a girl?" Dean flattened his palm across his chest.

Josh charged out of his chair like a bull, sending it raking across the linoleum floor.

The ag teacher stopped Josh just a hair off Dean's back. "That's enough." Then the teacher squeezed Dean around the back of his neck. "Don't say another word."

I dropped my head, partly because I was embarrassed and partly because Dean had gotten to me again. I'd moved on, but his slam still stung. Dean was right. Sundi Knutt had back-to-back prizewinning farm animals, a license to hunt, and cleavage—a mound of cleavage. That mound was the one obstacle I had no way of overcoming.

"Any other nominations?"

No one offered up anybody else. I was in. *Girls* or not, I was going to be the FFA Sweetheart, a hood ornament in the No-Jesus Christmas Parade. I perked back up. Sundi went beyond the call of good friend and shored up my position.

"Austin has worked really hard to get to know everyone. Her Bantam won first place at the fair, and she'll make a great representative." She put her hand on my shoulder. "So I nominate Austin Gray."

"I nominate Sundi Knutt," Dean blurted.

The room fell silent. I quit breathing.

"I said I nominate Sundi Knutt," Dean repeated.

Sundi took her hand off my shoulder and pressed it across her heart. She shook her blond curls and cooed, "I've already been sweetheart."

"So?" Dean threw his hands in the air.

I said nothing. I just sat still and turned blue.

Sundi looked at the teacher. "I can't possibly get it two years in a row."

Despite her leaving off the "can I?" part, Sundi's statement was more of a question, an appeal. Her big eyes twinkled with the possibility of being sweetheart again. For a hot moment, I could've skewered and roasted the marsh-mallow girl.

"We don't have any rules against it," the ag teacher ex-plained.

I inhaled, exhaled, tried to look indifferent. I checked the time on my wrist. No watch. I brushed imaginary dust off my sweater-covered flat chest. But I was dying. After everything I'd been through, becoming a hood ornament in the parade had come down to expecting Sundi, a natural-born sweetheart, to give up her title. No chance of that. It was in her blood.

"Done deal." Dean spit. "Sundi's the sweetheart."

No one argued. The notion of nominating forgotten.

Sundi bounced up. She had her arms locked behind her back, her girls prominent and projected. She twisted slightly from side to side like a little girl in Sunday school trying hard to recite her Bible verse. Every boy in class was hyp-notized by her.

At this point, I couldn't have gotten elected to watch the parade, much less be in it. Maybe I should've just signed up to grade dairy products at the State Fair: Austin Gray, Grand Champion Sour Milk Taster.

"I just want to say"—Sundi used her Little Bo Peep voice—"that Austin deserves to be sweetheart as much as I do. I'm still nominating Austin."

Good. This way I could get beat fair and square.

"Big deal. I'm still nominating Sundi." Dean flipped a pencil through his fingers.

"Anybody else?" The teacher picked up a handful of blank paper. He gave each student one sheet. "Write the name of the young lady you think best represents the FFA. Fold it and bring it to my desk."

Dean wrote real fast—SUNDI KNUTT in all caps. He walked backward to the teacher's desk, flashing his vote to everyone.

"I'll vote for you. You vote for me," Sundi whispered.

"You do that," I teased. "I'm voting for myself."

She squeezed my leg, then picked up a pen and started writing. "May the best girl win."

I knew who that would be.

off the curb

I stood on the curb looking in the window of Gray's True Value. The snow family was gone. The snow-daddy pulling the little snowgirl in the wagon, gone. The snowmomma, gone. It was Christmastime and the frosty front window of Gray's True Value displayed nothing but sheets of cottonlike fake snow. The Gray family tradition, gone.

I pushed open the door, stomped down the center aisle to the checkout counter. The store was empty. Charles Dickens was already in his coop. Momma closed early for the parade but would reopen afterward for late shopping. She was stacking plastic cups by a percolator full of hot cider.

"Where are they?" I wanted to kick something.

"Nice afternoon to you, too." Momma took off her reading glasses. She had been making changes, slowly. She finally sent the clothes in Daddy's closet to Goodwill, and she cleaned out the garage. Threw away a bunch of junk and boxed the rest. I didn't care about the clothes or the garage.

"What'd you do with the snow family?"

"Thought it was time for a new tradition." Momma pushed a stack of boxes from behind the counter. "With half the county coming downtown for the parade, I thought we'd debut this." She slit open a box with her pocketknife.

"You threw them out, didn't you?"

Momma closed the knife and tucked it back in her pocket. She scooted around the boxes, squared my shoulders, made me look at her.

"I would never throw something like that away, Austin." She held my face in her hands and wiped my tears with her thumbs. "We're taking the snow family home. We'll put a tree with lights and the snow family in the living room window. Decorate for the Christmas holidays for once. Give the neighbors something to talk about."

I tried not to smile and grabbed a Santa Claus napkin off the cider table.

"Is this really about the snow family?" Momma leaned against the counter. "Or is this about the parade?"

"I'm just so tired of loss." I dried the last of my tears. The FFA had named Sundi the sweetheart weeks ago; now the snow family was gone. Damn December. Losses piled up for me like Christmas wrapping paper scraps, leftover reminders of gifts given and taken away.

"The snow family is in my office. Like I said, it's going home with us." Momma filled a small cup with cider. "This is not a year of loss for us, Austin." The sweet cinnamon smell wafted through the store. "It's a beginning."

Momma took two short sips, put down her cup, and

reached into the brown box beside her. Styrofoam peanuts and bubble wrap spilled onto the floor. She pulled out a display-size elf—a funny-looking, dark-haired girl elf in an apron and holding a wooden spoon.

"Maribel?"

Momma chuckled and split open another box. Styrofoam peanuts piled around her feet. She cackled and gave me another girl elf. This one had on glossy black cowboy boots, a denim miniskirt, and was balancing a stack of wrapped packages.

"You did not!" I gasped at my self, elf image.

We tore into the rest of the boxes: little fake trees that lit up and blinked. A wooden structure, painted like the front of Gray's True Value, with a huge SANTA'S WORKSHOP sign. An elf in rectangle glasses with her hands on her hips. And one boy elf wearing a cowboy hat and sitting on a roll of wire.

"Wait until Raul sees that," I joked.

"There's one more." Momma dug around in the peanut mound. "What do you think of this?"

Momma handed me an ornate, near-perfect likeness of a Black Rosecomb Bantam with a Santa Claus hat tilted over the comb.

"Charles Dickens," I squealed.

"This year, this Christmas, is a beginning, Austin." Momma surveyed the store, the mess of boxes and Styrofoam. "No more looking back. No more icicle instead of mother." She started scooping the peanuts back into the boxes.

"Icicle?"

She'd been around Maribel too much.

"No more losing a part of myself every day. Waiting to drop." Momma stood up. Tiny bits of Styrofoam covered her sleeves and chest. "Too much time waiting on nothing." Momma shuffled through the peanuts and hugged me, squeezing me tight. "Don't do that, Austin. Don't waste time waiting around for life to happen to you. Make your own way."

Despite everything I'd done without her knowledge, permission, or approval, I knew from the strength of her hug that she meant it.

"Your daddy was a pro at living in the moment, reckless, but a pro. Spontaneous. If he wanted something, he just went and got it. His idea of planning was limited to making sure he had enough gas to get there."

Little by little, Momma brought my daddy back into the family.

I hopped onto the counter and let her finish.

"He'd find a way to make something happen. Like you did with the parade. *Momma, I want a chicken for Christmas*," she mimicked me. "You looked and sounded just like him. It scared me, Austin. Really scared me. And then the grappling!"

I rubbed my forearm. Nothing left of the scar but a thin, pink line.

"I worried that you were letting Dean Ottmer get to you, that you were losing confidence in yourself. But you seem to be over that." Momma raised her eyebrows as if she wasn't sure. "Don't ever let that happen. Don't let somebody rob you of that confidence, that flying down the highway, windows and radio wide-open confidence you got from your daddy."

The rat-a-tat-tat of snare drums buzzed into the store. The marching band was warming up.

"Austin." Momma held my elf likeness in her hand. "You should never be afraid to aspire to be like someone else. But you've got to be yourself first. Be your own icon." She stood the doll next to me on the counter, then stepped back with a nod of pure satisfaction. "And be it in your boots."

I could hear the trombones and trumpets tuning, so I hopped off the counter. "Momma, we'll have to put the workshop display together after the parade."

"I'll have a store full of customers!" She put her hands on her hips. Then I saw in her face that she knew. "Go ahead."

I kissed her cheek. "Watch for me!" I ran down the center aisle.

Tinsel-covered cars trimmed in Christmas lights lined the parade route. Trucks sporting glitter-covered signs pulled red-and-green decked-out floats.

"Go, Elvis!" I yelled at Lewis. He was leading the band in a plush, blue busby hat as tall as those the guards at Buckingham Palace wear. Lewis swung his baton around and blew his whistle. The band popped to attention. I followed the white stripe down the side of his uniform to the hem of his pants. Bell-bottoms. The Fortenberry Flare.

Josh and Sundi were in the parade lineup behind the UHOT board members this year. Sundi, poised on the hood, sparkled in a blue sequin halter dress.

I sneaked up to the side of the truck. "Flashy dress, Sweetheart."

"Hey-ey," she sang. "I'd hug you but I can't come down."

Josh lowered the passenger-side window. He was behind the wheel of one of Ottmer Ford's jet-black, jacked-up, spanking-new trucks.

I stood on my tiptoes and yelled up at Josh. "Did Dean deliver this to you?"

Dean had bragged for weeks about how his father would let the FFA use one of their trucks. He insisted on driving it, but Sundi cried and said she wasn't riding in the parade if Dean drove the truck.

"His father brought it to me." Josh kept one hand on the wheel, leaned across to the passenger window, and grinned. "Told me if Dean came near the truck to lock the doors and ignore him."

"Easy on the brakes or you'll toss the marshmallow girl!" I yelled.

He revved the engine. Sundi squealed and slapped at the windshield.

"Ride with him, Austin." Sundi leaned back on her hands, her soft hair lifting lightly in the breeze. She was a picture-perfect sweetheart. "Ride with him and make sure he doesn't stop quickly or try to do anything funny."

That would be completely out of character for Josh,

and Sundi knew it. But it gave her an opening, an opportunity to be a real sweetheart.

"Really? You want me to ride in the parade?"

"Of course." She batted her blue mascara-coated eyelashes and spread her glossed pink lips wide. "I should've thought about it sooner."

Mayor Nesmith's *Jesus Is The Reason For The Season* float cranked up behind us. His church members must've convinced him to let Jesus back into the Christmas parade. Nesmith, dressed as a shepherd and holding a staff, rode on the hood of a huge combine tractor. Farm equipment. The kind that separates wheat from chaff. The tractor pulled a trailer packed with little kids in fuzzy sheep suits. They sang "Silent Night" over and over.

"Get in!" Josh hollered as the UHOT car in front of him started down the parade route. He stretched across the cab and opened the door for me. I reached up for the handle, planted my right boot on the running board, and climbed in. High in the cab, I could see all over downtown Big Wells.

We rolled down Main Street. A little girl hugging her mother's leg took her thumb out of her mouth to wave at Sundi. She waved at me, too.

Josh was checking the rearview mirror.

"Look behind us," he said.

I glanced back. Nesmith, acting like the Pope, was blessing the crowd with his lame left hand. I cracked up. Only Nesmith could boil the Bible down to the simple message of *Just hang loose.*

We turned the corner by Gray's True Value. Momma had Santa's Workshop assembled and lit up in the window. She gave me two thumbs-up. Maribel stood beside her, sipping cider and waving with a sugar cookie.

Josh pulled my hand to him and clasped his fingers between mine.

I settled into the soft leather truck seat.

We passed between the lines of onlookers. A two-year-old in a red hooded jacket watched the parade from high on his father's shoulders. He waved at me with one hand, and stuck his finger up his nose with the other.

Inching along the old brick streets, I spotted Dean Ottmer on the corner. He cupped his hands around his mouth, yelling something his buddies thought was funny. Dean reminded me of a neglected yard dog stuck behind a fence, barking at any sign of life.

Then he saw me.

In the truck.

In the parade.

He shoved two of his friends and spit into the crowd. He hollered at me, but I didn't understand a word. It wouldn't have mattered if I could. Dean was about as significant to my life as a fart in a tornado. Dean didn't define me, nor did he leave me shaking in my boots. I blew him a kiss, which sent him into a rabid frenzy of more wild howling. "Somebody needs to slap a choke chain on that boy."

Josh laughed and shook his head. He rubbed his thumb

across mine, then kissed the back of my hand. "You're crazy, Austin."

I looked down. My hair fell in front of my face, and my cheeks warmed. I might be off center. And I was fine with that. Besides, Josh seemed to like a little unexpected in a girl.

From the truck window, I laughed as a group of giddy middle schoolers jumped into each other, trying to catch candy canes being tossed from floats. I failed to see the point of the struggle when every store around the square gave peppermints out after the parade. Then it hit me. It wasn't about the candy. The fun was in the experience.

When the kids cleared, an upright woman with silver helmet hair and a black mink coat appeared like some pious monument in front of the courthouse. She was studying Sundi's halter top as we rode by.

"Uh-oh." I squeezed Josh's hand and nodded out the window. "She's got party police written all over her."

The woman's face was screwed taut and I'd bet the farm that she was outlining a cleavage code for next year's parade. Sundi would be out of luck and I'd be in. A hood ornament in the No-Cleavage Christmas Parade. Yes, indeed.

Lewis Fortenberry had the Big Wells band going full blast. Old folks on the curb kept their hands smashed against their ears. Wanda from the Antique Mall stepped from her storefront for a better view. She was a plump woman, and in her green Christmas sweater and green stretchy pants, she looked like a gumdrop. Most of Prosper

County, from the downtown shop owners to the overalled farmers, huddled shoulder to shoulder, elbow to elbow, hip to hip, watching the parade.

"You know, Josh." I clicked the heels of my boots against the floorboard. "The curb is a crowded place."

Josh kissed the back of my hand again. He didn't say much. I liked that in a guy. Although I couldn't help but wonder just exactly what Josh Whatley had smoldering under his hood. Maybe he was working his way through something, too.

Rounding the square, I tapped the pointy toe of my boot as Lewis and the band played and swayed to Elvis's "Blue Christmas." Not a high mournful trumpet version, but a deep, swinging groove with honking tubas and bass drums. The parade watchers fell into the beat, clapping and rocking side to side. Sundi's wave even caught the rhythm and she bobbed her blond head.

For me, Christmas was no longer blue. And this little parade wasn't the end of the ride. I was just getting revved up.

acknowledgments

I am deeply grateful to the Society of Children's Book Writers and Illustrators, especially Kim Turrisi and Aaron Hartzler, for their efforts regarding conference manuscript critiques and their passionate commitment to great books for children. To my fantastic agent, Michael Bourret, I will always treasure your hearty laugh and sound advice. To my editor, Liz Szabla, thank you for the opportunity of a lifetime, as well as your steady hand through revisions and your constant enthusiasm for Austin and her journey. I'd trust you with my favorite muscle car.

My sincere thanks goes out to lots of folks around home: the best little critique group in Texas—Erin, Linda, Martha, and Sharon—for their unwavering support and sharp eyes; Sarah, Katie, Helen, Stacy, and Blake for their early reads and comments; the Shurbets and Alexanders, Harrisons and Bengtsons, for being the best of friends and family; and my son, William, whose sense of humor and laughter color my life and work.

Thanks, y'all.

Go Fish!

GO FISH

JILL S. ALEXANDER

What did you want to be when you grew up?
I didn't know what I wanted to be so much as I knew *where* I wanted to be. And that was *elsewhere*. In my little home community, professions included farmers and ranchers, teachers and preachers. I worked during my middle-school years at a truck stop located by an interstate. Folks like country music stars traveling between gigs in Little Rock and Dallas, and vacationing families in their *Brady Bunch* station wagons stopped in. I knew when I grew up, the first chance I got, I was going to check this country out. So I guess I wanted to be a traveler.

When did you realize you wanted to be a writer?
Being a writer is very different from being an author. I am a writer. I've written as far back as I can remember, and I think if I couldn't see or use my hands, I would still tell stories. For me, the transition to being an author was a conscious move from teaching English. After years of reading and sharing the works of others, I developed a yearning to put my own stories out there—to publish. I realized then that I wanted to be an author—to share the stories in my head with you.

What's your first childhood memory?
When I think back, my first memory is one more of setting than event. I think of my grandparents who helped raise me—a cool breeze floating through the screened windows of their old farmhouse, Nanny standing over a crock of fresh peaches soaked in sugar, and PawPaw shelling peas and singing crazy made-up songs to me like "She's long. She's tall. She's six feet from the ground."

What's your most embarrassing childhood memory?
Easter Sunday of my sixth-grade year, I left the bathroom and walked the length of the church aisle with the back of my dress tucked into my pantyhose. Yeah. Top that.

What's your favorite childhood memory?
Driving my first car—a candy apple red 1965 Mustang.

As a young person, who did you look up to most?
Johnny Cash. I loved the man and his music. When I was about twelve, we took a Griswald-like vacation to Tennessee and toured the outside of the Opry. Johnny Cash and June Carter were inside in the middle of a dress rehearsal. Despite the fact that we didn't have the money to go in, they let us watch anyway. I have a picture of Johnny and June (with her hair in rollers) from that day. It is my prized possession and sits on my desk.

What was your worst subject in school?
Math and all its horrible versions: algebra, geometry, fractions, stupid decimal stuff.

What was your best subject in school?
Homemaking. Yes, we had that and they actually called it that. Girls took homemaking. Boys took something called Bachelor

Living. We cooked mostly. I was a whiz thanks to my grand-mother and my truck stop diner experience.

What was your first job?
In middle school, I bussed tables at the local truck stop and a catfish restaurant called the Hushpuppy. In high school, I worked for Mason's True Value Hardware on the downtown square in Mt. Pleasant, Texas. Loved that job. The store inspired Gray's hardware in *The Sweetheart of Prosper County*.

How did you celebrate publishing your first book?
I'm still celebrating. *does Snoopy dance again*

Where do you write your books?
A comfy plaid chair in the corner of my den.

Where do you find inspiration for your writing?
My ideas come from getting out and about, meeting people. I have a particular sensitivity to ironic contrasts.

Which of your characters is most like you?
I think you'll always find headstrong, independent girls in a story of mine. Wherever they show up, that's a little bit of me coming through. I don't know how to write "Poor me, I need to be rescued."

When you finish a book, who reads it first?
I actually have two readers: my niece, Sarah, and my friend Stacy. They're both voracious readers and honest critiquers. I also have a fantastic critique group of other writers who read a chapter here and there as I'm writing.

Are you a morning person or a night owl?
Hoot! Hoot! Going with night owl definitely.

What's your idea of the best meal ever?
Thanksgiving lunch with my family. Comfort food and my folks.
Pass the gravy.

Which do you like better cats or dogs?
Horses.

What do you value most in your friends?
Honesty. And my friend Stacy has a sweet boat.

Where do you go for peace and quiet?
My car.

What makes you laugh out loud?
Playing Scrabble with my family. None of them can spell.

What's your favorite song?
"The Night the Lights Went Out in Georgia" rocked my world
when I first heard it back in the seventies. My grandmother
taught me to write by copying down the lyrics.

Who is your favorite fictional character?
I really love Scout in *To Kill a Mockingbird.* Kindred spirit.

What are you most afraid of?
I'm pretty fearless. Being Jesus-y has its advantages.

What time of year do you like best?
Fall. I find intoxicating the cooling down from a hot summer, the
burst of autumn colors, and football. Tailgating anyone? Oh,

and pumpkins—Cinderella pumpkins, fairy-tale pumpkins, the traditional jack-o'-lantern—I love them all.

What is your favorite TV show?
Friday Night Lights. And I'm a sucker for CMT videos.

If you were stranded on a desert island, who would you want for company?
My brother. He is a Boy Scout and an engineer. We'd be sailing for home in a handmade raft in no time.

If you could travel in time, where would you go?
Do I have cash or no? If I'm loaded? Fitzgerald's New York. If I'm broke? Thoreau's Walden.

What's the best advice you've ever received about writing?
I live and write by the mantra "Tell the story only you can tell."

What do you want readers to remember about your books?
When folks think of *Prosper County*, I'd like for them to be reminded that no matter who you are or where you are or what your obstacles may be, the power to course an inspired and hope-filled life lives within every individual.

What would you do if you ever stopped writing?
I don't think I can stop writing, telling stories. However, being an author is a privilege. If my opportunities as an author end, I'll probably teach English by day and pout by night.

What do you like best about yourself?
I enjoy life. Not that I don't have moments of anger or sadness, I just don't lie down and wallow in them. My family never put up with a lot of moping. Whenever I got upset, my mother would say, "Well, you've got the same britches to be glad in."

What is your worst habit?
Twitter.

What do you consider to be your greatest accomplishment?
My accomplishments are not my own. I can do nothing apart from Christ, and I am greatly blessed to have amazing people in my life. I have an education, thanks to my husband. I had a successful teaching career, thanks to my students. I have a terrific debut novel, thanks to an outstanding publishing team.

Where in the world do you feel most at home?
I am at home wherever my family is. My family is my home. The rest is just logistics.

What do you wish you could do better?
I'm always working to improve my own writing. I love the craft. Still, there is much to learn.

What would your readers be most surprised to learn about you?
The shocking truth is I'm really just a mom. *waves from the top of the football stadium*

Keep reading for an excerpt from

Paradise by Jill S. Alexander

coming soon in hardcover from Feiwel and Friends.

All it took to find Paradise was a five-dollar bill
and an ad in the *Thrifty Nickel*.

WANTED
Frontman for country rock band.
Good vocals. NO guitar players.
Auditions Thursday
CR 218, Cross the RR tracks, 1st left after peach grove

I was shocked, really, that the ad worked. For starters, cutting out all guitar players whittled the already-small field down to a nub. Most singers at some point in time had picked up a guitar. But Waylon, who considered himself anointed country music royalty by right of his first name, never listened to reason. As a matter of fact, Waylon Slider didn't care what I thought as long as I showed up after school with my drumsticks and opened up my Uncle L.V.'s airplane hangar to rehearse.

We'd been playing to the Piper Cub and the Miss Molly Moonlight, painted on the nose of the old World War II–bomber, for about an hour when Waylon put down his six-string and snatched up the want ads. His rusty, reddish-brown hair mounded around his head in a tangled bird's nest of coarse curls. Sitting on his stool with a fistful of the *Thrifty Nickel*, Waylon looked like a pouty little Tom Sawyer in time-out. He raked his top teeth across his bottom lip and pinched his bushy eyebrows together like he just couldn't make out why no one had answered the ad.

I twisted a bit on my stool, practicing a drumstick toss and backhanded catch. "You know, putting *NO* in all caps made us look like we had a bunch of insecure guitarists."

"Shut up, Paisley!" He rolled the *Thrifty Nickel* into a club and reared up. If I'd been a boy, I think he would have hit me. But he mumbled *dumb blonde* instead and sat back down. "You don't know anything about band management. Nobody cares what you think."

That last part was truer than he knew. But with Texa-palooza just three months away, my shot at playing on the same stage as some of the best drummers in the state seemed to be slipping away. The Waylon Slider Band needed a lead singer. So far, Waylon Slider had managed to screw it up.

A gust of March wind blasted the metal siding of the hangar walls like an echoing gong. Cal unplugged his lead guitar. Levi cased his bass.

I had left the tall, sliding doors slightly open on the west side, the pasture side of the hangar. The evening sun hung just above the pine thicket in the distance, sending a rectangle of orange light between the doors and glinting off the chrome on my snare.

"Waylon." I stood up, tugging at the frayed edges of my cutoff shorts. "I've got to close up and be through the woods before it gets dark and cold. There's always tomorrow. We'll find someone."

I reached for the tarp to hide my drums when the sunlight went black. Afraid I might have misjudged the time, I spun around. Faced the doors.

Filling the gap was a tall figure in a wide-brimmed hat. He stood with his feet apart and something slung over his shoulder like a saddlebag. Eclipsing the light, he looked like a cowboy cutout etched onto the setting sun.

Waylon jumped to his feet. "You're not here about the ad, are you?"

The boy didn't say anything. He ambled across the concrete floor with a bronc-busting swagger like he'd just gone eight seconds on Boom-Shocka-Locka. He pulled up in front of Waylon, and cocked his head at Cal and Levi. The boy caught me in his crosshairs, honing in first on my denim cutoffs, then my boots.

I reached into my back pocket. Pulled out my drumsticks. I tossed one into my left hand and twirled the other by my side. Just to let him know I was more than eye candy and the role of band badass was taken.

He grinned, and when he did, the smooth center of his left cheek dimpled.

I dropped my drumstick. Slipping from badass to dumb-ass in a heartbeat.

The boy watched it bounce and spin onto the floor. Then he gave Waylon a fist bump and said, "I sing some."

"Sweet. 'Cause we don't." Levi rolled the toothpick dangling off his lip from one corner of his mouth to the other. "*Some* will be an improvement."

Waylon's freckled face turned pink. It wrenched his gut that his voice slipped into a nasal honk when his nerves got the best of him. He grabbed his six-string by the neck. "You don't play guitar, right?"

The boy in the cowboy hat rubbed his hand over the strap of his bag. "Naw, man. Guitar's not my thing."

The flesh tone came back to Waylon's face. Since competition on guitar was all he seemed to care about, and Levi was willing to let a dog howl while we played as long as we got to play, it was up to me and Cal to check this guy out. I looked to Cal for some help, but he was bent over his spiral, hidden under his long hair, scribbling furiously.

I was going to have to ask the questions, and the light outside was growing dim. We were running out of time.

"Look," I started. I had never seen him before, so he was either new or went to one of the surrounding county schools. "Not to be rude, but I've got to lock up. So, who are you and where are you from?"

His black hat shaded his eyes, but I noticed that he had small gold loops in each earlobe. He wore a plaid snap shirt with the sleeves rolled up and cinched around his biceps.

And the hem of his faded jeans was slit at the seams, probably to make it easier to fit over his boots.

"I'm Gabe." That dimple on his left cheek winked. "From Paradise."

Cal glanced up, shaking the hair away from his face.

Levi laughed and slapped both hands on his knees. "Well, dude, you're in for major disappointment, 'cause we ain't seen a chick in a coconut bra and a grass skirt since Halloween."

So much for professionalism.

"He means Texas," Waylon blurted. "Paradise, Texas, right?"

"Sure." The boy swung his bag from one shoulder to the other like he was toting a fifteen-pound sack of potatoes.

"Waylon." I tucked my sticks back into my pocket and threw the tarp over my drums. The ting of the cymbals rang through the hangar like the starting bell for the water gun race at the Prosper County Fair. "Paradise has three minutes to prove he can sing."

"She's not joking," Waylon told him. "Sing something. Anything. Quick."

The last sliver of sunlight slipped into the hangar, reaching across the black-tarped drum set and touching the silver ring on my left hand.

With one knee slightly bent, the boy from Paradise tapped the heel of his boot against the floor three times — counting himself in. Then he growled out a husky, Johnny Cash version of "This Little Light of Mine."

Before he could finish off the last *Let it shine* and I could say *You've got to be kidding*, Levi started clapping. He stopped long enough to take the toothpick out of his mouth and announce, "Good enough for me."

Waylon's face lit up. He raised his eyebrows at me and I gave in. The raspy, low tone of the boy's voice could add an edge to our sound. And he could stay on pitch. Even if he couldn't, Gabe from Paradise was our only hope.

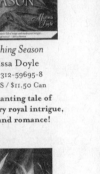
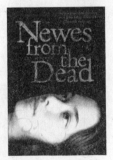

Six chilling tales

AVAILABLE FROM SQUARE FISH

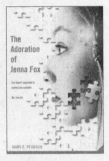

The Adoration of Jenna Fox
Mary E. Pearson
ISBN: 978-0-312-59441-1
$8.99 US / $11.50 Can

*What happened to Jenna Fox?
And who is she, really?*

The Compound
S.A. Bodeen
ISBN: 978-0-312-57860-2
$8.99 US / $11.50 Can

*Eli's father built the Compound to
keep his family safe. But are they
safe—or sorry?*

Dead Connection
Charlie Price
ISBN: 978-0-312-37966-7
$7.99 US / $10.25 Can

*Can Murray's ability to talk
to dead people help him find
a missing cheerleader?*

Holdup
Terri Fields
ISBN: 978-0-312-56130-7
$8.99 US / $11.50 Can

*The most dangerous thing at Burger
Heaven should be greasy food,
not a maniac with a gun.*

The Love Curse of the Rumbaughs
Jack Gantos
ISBN: 978-0-312-38052-6
$7.99 US / $8.99 Can

*Ivy has two great loves, her mother
and taxidermy.*

Zombie Blondes
Brian James
ISBN: 978-0-312-57375-1
$8.99 US / $11.50 Can

*All of the girls in Hannah's
new school are blonde and
popular—and dead.*